SEAL OF APPROVAL

CYNTHIA TERELST

ISBN: 978-0-6487294-7-1

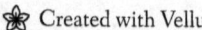 Created with Vellum

Thanks for choosing Seal of Approval to escape in. It's a privilege being able to share my work with you.

Being an author can sometimes be a lonely endeavour, unless my cats decide to visit me while I'm writing. But knowing there are awesome readers like you turning the pages helps me feel a part of something bigger.

CHAPTER ONE

Jasmine

Rose crossed her arms and dropped onto the couch. Nine years of stubbornness flashed in her blue eyes. "I'm not sharing a room with him." She threw a piercing glare at her brother.

Bailey's head whipped in her direction, his mouth opening to offer a retort.

I sighed, cutting him off. "You have no choice. The new ranger, Ethan, is arriving in two days."

Being a mum was hard sometimes, and *this* was one of those times. How many repetitions of this same conversation did we need to have?

"Why does he have to live here?" Rose's arms tightened across her chest.

Bailey rolled his eyes skyward. If they lifted any higher, they'd hit the ceiling. My lips quirked. Rose stilled them with a pointed stare.

"The house Ethan was moving into is being renovated and isn't ready yet."

Rose could be as stubborn as she wanted, but it wouldn't change the fact that the new part-time ranger would soon be sharing our house. I didn't like it either. I liked our peaceful life and the easy routine we'd built over the last five years since we'd moved here.

"Why can't he live somewhere else?" Rose said.

"It's tourist season. All the other houses are taken."

The only movement from either child came from Bailey, whose glare switched from his sister to me. I wasn't going to be ambushed by an eleven-year-old and a nine-year-old.

"You either help me move your stuff or I'll do it myself." I walked off towards Bailey's bedroom. "If you don't like where I put everything, that's your problem." Five metres out from the bedroom, and there was no movement behind me. Two metres. Nothing. I reached the doorway and stepped inside. As I tied my long brown hair into a ponytail, Bailey arrived at my side. I smiled to myself. I knew calling their bluff would work. There was no way he'd want me to mess up his stuff.

"I know it will be squishy, but hopefully Ethan won't have to stay long," I said.

I turned back to the couch. Rose was still there, not willing to admit defeat yet. She would. As soon as we started moving things into her room.

"We'll need to move your bookcase and books into the living room," I said to Bailey. "And Rose's too," I added loud enough for her to hear, "so your bed will fit."

Rose ran to her room. "I'll move my books. They have to go in the exact same order."

I left them with that task and started to move Bailey's clothes. I knew exactly how they felt about Ethan moving in. Head office thought Ethan moving in with us, rather than living in Somewhere Bay thirty minutes away, was ideal. I didn't think having our space invaded by a stranger was ideal. They wanted him close so he could learn and have easy access to the sea lions for his research. They never explained exactly what that research would be. But according to them, I needed to help him in any way I could.

There was no point arguing. We lived in a government-provided house rent-free as part of my employment package. The house next door would be part of Ethan's package. Him living with us would save them on unnecessary rental fees and travel expenses until the renovations on his house were complete.

They were adamant the renovations would be finished soon. They wouldn't listen when I told them they'd hardly been started. It looked like I was going to need to project manage it if it was going to happen at all.

They may have been completely disorganised on that front, but I knew that their hiring protocols were strict. They were a government department, after all. They wouldn't hire anyone with a criminal record. In fact, you couldn't even get into Australia if you had a criminal record, so at least we were safe on that front. They'd emailed me his name this morning so I would do some more research before he arrived; just to make sure. You can't hide on the internet. If he was sketchy, I would find it.

"Finished, Mummy," Rose said. She'd lined her books up on her bed.

"Go get the beach cart. It will be easier to move the books."

She ran off.

"Bailey, can you help me move the bookcase, please?"

Within seconds, he was there.

Rose supervised as we moved her bookcase. "I want my

books closer to the door so the mermaids can get to the books easier when they want to read."

"Because an extra metre is really going to hurt them," Bailey said.

Rose huffed. "They don't have legs, you know."

"They—"

I pushed Bailey in the direction of his room. "Your bookcase, now." We did not need a discussion about mermaids and their anatomy or their ability to read.

Once the bookcases were in place, they started to put their books away talking with each other the whole time.

"Finished, Mummy," Rose said, appearing in her doorway.

"Bailey, too?"

"Yes."

"Good job. Go play on the beach while I go to the store to ask Jack for help with the bigger furniture."

I walked along the beach to the general store. The sea breeze played at the tendrils of hair that had escaped from my ponytail. It was unusually warm for October, hinting at the hot summer that was soon to come. I made a mental note to check the fire trails over the next week.

The holiday homes to my right overlooked the sandy beach and the bay to my left. Some were big, others small. The larger houses were double-storey, with large windows taking in the view. They were modern and rendered in natural colours to blend in with the bush behind.

They were interspersed with smaller houses, almost like fisherman shacks. These timber houses had paint peeling from years of exposure to the sea. Although they weren't as grand, they were no less popular with tourists.

Only a one-lane dirt road separated the buildings from

the bush behind. The lane allowed access when the road out the front flooded in a king tide.

The campground that straddled the beach was no less popular. Grey nomads in their caravans and motorhomes inhabited it, even in the cold winter months. The younger travellers used tents while families often packed into camper trailers.

The water was calm, tiny waves lapping at the shore.

The one-kilometre walk did me good. Bailey and Rose had hardly stopped bickering all afternoon. Even Timmy, their four-month-old ginger kitten, had left them, seeking solace on my bed.

This had better not be a sign of things to come. Our peace had already been shattered before Ethan even arrived. Living with Ethan would be nothing like living with Max, Rose and Bailey's father. I'd make sure of that. There was no way my children would feel uncomfortable in their own home. That's one reason I'd moved Bailey into Rose's room. It was closer to me, and it would give Ethan space to himself at the other end of the house.

I made my way up the steps to the front door of the store. Soft sand had accumulated under the stairs. Jack would need to clear it out before the treads were overcome with a carpet of the small particles.

The bell clinked as I entered. Jack's weathered face turned toward me and broke into a smile. "What brings you here on this fine afternoon?"

"I was wondering if you could help me move Bailey's bed into Rose's room, please? And some furniture from the house next door into the new ranger's room."

Lily popped out from one of the aisles. Her greying, curly hair framed her face. "Preparing for your American co-worker?"

I leant against the counter. "He arrives in two days. I thought it would be a good idea for the kids to get used to their new living arrangements before then."

Jack's blue eyes twinkled. "And how is that going?"

I looked out the window to the beach where the kids were playing. "Well, they haven't killed each other yet."

Lily laughed. "I hope it doesn't come to that. Do you have a name for your new co-worker?"

I pulled out my phone and scrolled to the email. "They emailed it this morning. Ethan Shaw. Marine biologist. Splits his time between Monterey Bay Aquarium and the university."

Lily came to stand beside her husband. "Ooh, high level. Do you have a picture?"

I shook my head. "If you've seen one middle-aged man, you've seen them all."

Jack puffed out his chest. "Some of us are finer specimens than others."

I laughed.

Lily took out her phone and tapped away. A cheeky smile lit up her face. She showed her husband whatever was on her phone.

He slapped his leg, chuckled and gave her a nudge. "That is no ordinary middle-aged white man."

"Not ordinary." She waggled her eyebrows. "And not middle-aged."

What were they talking about? I hadn't had time to google him yet. Were we about to get stuck with some grumpy old guy? Lily handed her phone to me. I sucked in a breath. Oh, shit. The person staring into the camera was mid-thirties and had a smile as captivating as his hazel eyes. They seemed to see right through the centre of me in every photo I flipped through. He wasn't even here in person yet and already I found it hard to tear my eyes away. My mouth went dry. I scrolled. He looked as good in a dress shirt as he did in a wetsuit peeled off to his waist.

"You're shitting me." My eyes went to the search bar: Ethan Shaw, Marine Biologist. I shoved the phone back into Lily's hand.

"Too hot to handle, huh?" Jack asked, chortling.

"Have fun knowing that fine specimen, or should we call him *Sex on Legs*, is sleeping only metres away." Lily gave me a wink.

"Co-worker, housemate, that's it."

I wiped the images from my mind. Or at least I tried to.

Two more days until Ethan arrived. I didn't know if I wanted his charm to match his good looks or the opposite. Which would be better?

CHAPTER TWO

Ethan

I WAS five hours into my drive from Adelaide to Haven Bay. The towns on the dusty highway were few and far between, each one smaller than the last. Trees with tall, thick trunks and branches, and a head of leaves reminded me of gangly teenagers.

I'd asked my phone for information about the area as I drove, and it told me this was a wheat farming area. The soil here didn't look like it would sustain much life. It was pale and dry. But what would I know? My life was on the water, not the land. I studied the horizon. The land was as flat as the sea on a calm day. Nothing like San Francisco with its continuous hills. Everyone who lived there knew where to walk or bike to avoid the hills. It's a skill well learned.

I pulled into a gas station and a man in his fifties with a cap pulled down low on his head came out. I hopped out of the car and headed to the pump.

"I'll do that for you, mate," he said as he reached me.

I handed the nozzle over. It was rare to get this service back home.

"Where ya heading?" he asked as he started pumping the gas.

"Haven Bay. I'll be working there for six months."

He gave a low whistle. "That's out woop woop."

"Woop woop?"

"Yeah, beyond the black stump."

What black stump? Was there some famous black stump I should know about? Nothing I'd read had mentioned it. I must have looked confused, because the man cracked a grin. "It means the middle of nowhere."

"Oh, right." Of course, it did. They had weird sayings here. Like calling the truck I was driving a ute.

"Somewhere Bay is the closest town to it. Decent-sized town. Half-hour drive."

I cocked my head. It was a strange name for a town.

The man chuckled. "I get that look a lot when I say the name. The ship that explored those waters had no idea where they were. So, they called it Somewhere Bay."

I nodded. When I'd googled Haven Bay, all I'd found was that it was situated close to a national park and a marine park. I didn't pay much attention to the surrounding area, including *Somewhere Bay*. The sea lions were what I was interested in.

"What are ya going to be doing there?" he asked as the nozzle clicked in his hand.

"I'll be studying the sea lion colony. I'm a marine biologist."

He nodded and headed inside. I followed. "Popular tourist thing, that. They have tours taking people to swim with the sea lions."

I had read about the tours and tried to withhold my

reservations until I saw them in action myself. My first reaction was negative. It sounded like something that would disturb the natural order.

I handed over my credit card and paid for the gas before heading back to the truck. When I pulled out onto the road, I made sure I was driving on the left-hand side. It was easier to remember when I was in traffic and just followed the flow.

I'd done plenty of research on the sea lions, but obviously not enough on the area itself. I hadn't realised that it was so remote. It didn't matter, it was the sea lions I was interested in. And six months in *woop woop* was well worth the sacrifice. I had a lot planned, and it all revolved around my research. I was leaving nothing behind in the States except my job, but that was being held open for my return.

The six months I'd be spending on this research project was the last thing I needed to complete my dissertation to get my PhD. This would open the door to me becoming a professor and furthering my research.

I took the turnoff to Haven Bay onto a dirt road, smooth in some areas and bumpy in others. There were low shrubs on both sides. These plants were well adapted to the sandy soil and salt air. Low to protect them from the wind, with small spindly leaves that conserved water because there was less surface area for evaporation.

As I drove towards the town, the land on my right thinned until the road was only fifty feet from the water. Pristine white sand stretched down to beautiful, calm blue water. It was nothing like most of the beaches in San Francisco, which were rocky and cliffy. I opened the window, allowing the salty air to fill the cabin.

The classification of the middle of nowhere was correct. There were no buildings or manmade structures in sight.

No cars or humans. Finally, I reached the town of Haven Bay.

There wasn't much to see. Twenty or so houses hugged the road further along. I passed a general store. It was two floors, probably the store on the bottom level and living quarters upstairs. A man and woman were clearing sand from the front stairs with a broom and shovel. They waved as I drove past.

Opposite this was a jetty where a boat was moored. The words on the side said *South Australian Land Management*.

A café came next, the sign advertising the best fish and chips from Friday to Monday. It was a small building with tables and chairs out the front. A small shop that offered equipment hire for the beach and camping, and doggy day care followed. Smart. Tourists could visit the national park and leave their dogs somewhere safe.

The last building before the row of houses was a small office attached to a large shed. The sign out the front read *South Australian Land Management Ranger*. This would be the office I would share with the other ranger.

The instructions I'd received were to drive to the last house. I was looking forward to settling in and getting myself set up. I could keep my research and laptop in one place for a change and spread it out for easy access. Splitting my time between the university and the aquarium had meant living in two places and transporting what I needed from one place to the other. Here, it would be different.

As I pulled into the driveway of a small house and parked, two brown-haired children zoomed out, followed by an orange kitten. A woman appeared in the doorway and yelled something about the kitten. The young boy turned, picked the kitten up and kept running all in one fluid motion. The woman blew her long hair out of her face and spun to go back inside. Her eyes caught sight of the car and froze when they landed on me.

I sat rooted to my spot as I took her in. Her long brown hair complemented her long tanned legs. Her short t-shirt revealed a hint of golden skin at her midriff. Words swam through my head——wild, free, calm, confident, beautiful, strong, gentle, familiar, enduring—and I tried to grasp one that would best portray her—untamed. Like the ocean.

What was she doing at the house I was supposed to be living in?

CHAPTER THREE

Jasmine

My BREATHING FALTERED as hazel eyes stared back at me. I'd recognise Ethan anywhere, just by his eyes alone. His pictures flashed through my mind. I shoved them away and descended the stairs as the car door opened and Ethan stepped out. He was wearing shorts and a polo, the exposed skin well-tanned.

As I approached him, his eyes wandered to the yard and house. What was he noticing? The kids' bikes, the small garden, the hammock on the porch? Was he trying to ignore my wild appearance—messy hair, flour on my t-shirt, bare feet? It was hard to tell what he thought. His face was impassive. At least I was wearing a bra.

"Hi. You must be Ethan. I'm Jasmine. I'm the head ranger here." I held my hand out to him. "Nice to meet you."

A half smile appeared as he took my hand and shook it. His was big and warm but as non-committal as his face—no firm squeeze, no lingering. The handshake finished as quickly as it started. Still, I couldn't read him. My stomach squeezed. It was part of my job to read people, to recognise whether they were genuine. I met all kinds of people as a ranger. Some were merely out enjoying nature; others were there to exploit it.

I squared my shoulders, preparing myself. "Have head office explained the housing situation to you?"

He shook his head.

I took a steadying breath. "The house next door is yours."

His eyes drifted to the house. The doors were wide open and old cabinetry was sitting on the grass. Wood and sawhorses covered the porch. Rubbish stuck out the top of the skip bin.

"Unfortunately, it's undergoing renovations. Until they finish, you'll need to share with us."

His eyes widened almost imperceptibly. Mmm, so he *can* show emotion.

I led him toward our house. "We have set up a room for you. I hope you'll find it comfortable." I took him there first. Jack and I had moved the queen bed, two side tables and a chest of drawers in from next door. I'd hoped that would be enough for him.

"This looks fine. Thanks."

"It used to be my son's, Bailey's, room. He's moved in with Rose. They're adjusting to sharing a room, so some days it's a little crazy." I tried to make my voice light. I didn't want him to think he was moving into a madhouse.

"Right. OK."

Was he being dismissive? Or sarcastic, like he thought we were always crazy? I straightened my back. Why was I being so defensive? The poor man had just driven seven hours. He was probably tired. And then he was faced with having to share a house with three strangers.

I led him down the hall to the bathroom, conscious that his eyes were on me the whole way. "This bathroom will be yours. The kids and I will share the other bathroom."

"Thanks."

"The other two bedrooms are down that way," I said, pointing down the hall. "And this is the living area. I didn't know if you'd want to share meals or make your own. We can make space for you in the fridge and pantry. Let me know your preference once you've settled in."

He nodded. He didn't say much. He merely looked at me with those intense hazel eyes. Maybe ten words during our whole conversation, while all I'd done was ramble on. Did he think this was as awkward as I did?

I hoped it was shock on his part that made him so aloof. I didn't want the kids to feel uneasy. I wanted them to be free to express themselves. They hadn't been free with Max. His judgement had reigned supreme. Little by little, I'd seen their self-esteem erode. They had begun to overthink everything they said. I wouldn't allow that to happen again.

I showed him the laundry and the small backyard. "There is a road that leads to the back of the house as well." I pointed it out. "We use it if the beach road out the front is impassable for some reason."

He ran his hand through his hair and looked around. There was a small crease between his eyebrows, indicating he was thinking about something. He nodded and gave me that half smile again. "Thank you."

That half smile showed me that while he may have been fighting with other emotions, he was trying.

My defences had me jumping to conclusions. And that

wasn't fair on either of us. Hopefully, he would relax and this whole experience could at least be bearable. Especially since we'd be living together and working together.

Maybe he had a family back home and living with us would make him miss them more. Or maybe he was an introvert who liked his own space. He was here for six months, but he wouldn't need to live with us that whole time if I could get all the tradesmen sorted.

What could I do to make this better for all of us?

CHAPTER FOUR

Ethan

I NEEDED SPACE. I needed to get my head around these living arrangements. The last woman I'd shared a house with was my wife, now ex-wife. She'd left five years ago. And kids? My brother had two but I had none of my own. His house was like bedlam some days. I imagined it was the same here with those two kids I saw earlier.

Uncomfortable didn't begin to describe how I was feeling. If you added in a little fear, that'd be closer to the mark. I'd never had children for a reason. I liked them well enough. But being a father was not in the cards for me. Not with my father's genes running through my blood.

"Would you like a tour of the town?" Jasmine asked after she finished showing me around the house. She smiled, but her serious brown eyes were studying me. I shifted my weight from one foot to the other.

"No, that's OK. I'll just go for a short walk to stretch my legs."

She nodded. "Well, you can't get lost. There's only one road in and out."

I made my way down the stairs. Directly across the dirt road was a sandy beach. And beyond that the bay stretched into the distance, the water a soft fusion of dark blue and azure. It was a stunning October day—sunny with a slight breeze that didn't chill to the bone. I absorbed it all, tension leaving my shoulders. I glanced back at the porch. It looked like it was set up to enjoy the scenery and ambience, with chairs looking out over the beach and a hammock as well.

I was certain Jasmine was a single mom. She hadn't mentioned a partner and the photos I'd seen on the living room wall were of her and the two children. Did it matter? I didn't know. She made me uncomfortable. It wasn't anything she'd done specifically. Perhaps it was the way she looked at me like I was a specimen whenever she spoke.

I laughed to myself. I'd been accused of the same thing many a time. I always thought it was because of the scientist in me. According to the department, Jasmine wasn't a scientist though. What was she trying to figure out?

This housing situation was not ideal. How was I going to conduct my research and complete my dissertation under these conditions? There was no space here for me to have a permanent set up. Maybe I could squeeze a desk into my room. That would give me some sort of separation from the rest of the house at least. I nodded to myself as I kept walking.

A young woman with blonde hair up in a messy bun was setting out flags next to the café as I passed. She gave me a wave and a smile. The two people at the general store were finished with their sand duty. I walked up the stairs, curious to see what the one store in town sold. Light laughter flitted up from the beach. I glanced over my shoulder. The two children from earlier were running across the sand with the kitten.

The bell above the door rang as I entered. The man at the counter lifted his eyes from the newspaper he was reading. A peal of laughter followed me through the door. His attention turned to the children, looking at them with a small smile before his gaze settled back on me. "How can I help you today?"

"I was just curious to see what you sell," I told him.

He inclined his chin. "Ethan Shaw? The new ranger?"

"Yes." How did he know?

"Lily," he called out toward the back of the shop. "Come and meet Ethan." He turned to me and gestured out the window. "You'll never have a dull moment with those two."

I imagined not. They seemed as free as the sea breeze that tugged at their brown hair. The boy—Bailey?—lifted the kitten onto a paddle board on the sand and swayed it from side to side. The kitten lowered its centre of gravity, stabilising itself. Once it had had enough, it jumped off. The boy gave it a gentle pat.

"Rose had her heart set on a kitten," a woman said. "So, they got Timmy. That kitten hardly leaves their side."

Rose placed the kitten on the board next, under the watchful eye of her brother. They were a lot calmer now than when I'd first seen them.

"I'm Lily," the woman said, drawing my attention to her. Her curly greying hair and ready smile helped me relax. "And this is my husband, Jack. I bet he forgot to introduce himself."

"Ethan. Nice to meet you both."

Jack faced his wife. "Ethan came in to see what we stock."

"I'll give you the shortest tour in the name of short tours," she said.

Lily walked me through the shop, telling me about the different products. It wasn't large—two short aisles with shelves.

"We don't hold much stock. There are only ten permanent residents in town. We do our shopping in Somewhere Bay."

That made sense.

"We stock what we find the tourists are most in need of. Grey nomads like to support small local businesses, so we make sure we cater to them. We have a small book section where Jack sells his second-hand books."

I cocked my head. "Grey nomads?"

"Retirees, travelling around Australia. We call them grey nomads because they're older and often have grey hair."

I nodded and glanced at the shelves as we walked past. There was long-life milk, pasta, toiletries, snacks. The freezer had bread, fries and vegetables.

"Sara lives next door. She's a part-time teacher in Somewhere Bay and operates the fish and chip shop here. It's very popular. We all have a bonfire once a week with fish and chips and people travel all the way from Somewhere Bay to join us. Plus, there's always the tourists and campers."

It sounded like a nice sense of community. And an inclusive one too, if tourists were welcomed.

"Ross and Jay are in the next shop over. Ross is a doctor in Somewhere Bay. Jay runs the shop and doggy day care. They've been married for five years. No children yet, but they're working on it. Adoption is hard in Australia, so they're looking into surrogacy."

It was weird that everyone knew everything about each other. In San Francisco, you could live a completely anonymous life. How much would the town inhabitants know about me by the end of the day? What would Jasmine tell them?

"It will be strange for Jasmine and the children to have someone living with them," Lily said as we returned to the front counter, confirming that Jasmine was a single mom. It would be strange for me too. I wasn't going to tell Lily that, though.

How much would Jasmine expect me to integrate with their lives? Not much, I hoped. All I wanted to do was complete the next step in earning my doctorate.

CHAPTER FIVE

Jasmine

I SERVED dinner and took my place at the table. Bailey had hardly spoken a word since he'd gotten home. He glanced at Ethan furtively and then back at his plate. Ethan was the perfect reflection of Bailey. Was he always this quiet?

"Meat pie, my favourite," Rose said, grinning. She poked at the golden flaky pastry, nodding with satisfaction. Then she screwed her nose up at the vegetables. "They're not my favourite."

"Eat them first then," I suggested, like I always did.

"But what if I run out of room and miss out on my pie? That would be a tragedy."

I laughed. Tragedy was her new favourite word. It was amazing how many things could be a tragedy in a nine-year-old's life.

"Do you like meat pies, Ethan?" she asked.

"Yes. We call them pot pies in America."

Bailey's eyes narrowed. "Why?"

I smiled to myself. Curiosity would always drive Bailey

to open up. Even if it was just a simple question like this. He was what I called a whale learner. A whale opens its mouth to take in all the water in its path. Bailey was the same with learning. He opened his mind to everything and took it all in. He may have been nervous about Ethan's presence, but that didn't stop his question.

"They used to be cooked in pots."

A crease formed between Bailey's eyebrows, but he didn't ask any more questions. He started eating his vegetables. He would google that later. And down a rabbit hole, he would go.

Ethan picked up his knife and fork and cut into the pie.

Rose stared at him, her blue eyes intense. "Is that how you eat pies in America?"

"Yes." Ethan glanced around the table. We were all watching him, our knives and forks beside our plates.

"We eat pies with our hands," Rose said. She picked up her pie. "If you're really talented like Jack, you can eat it with one hand. When he was younger, he could eat a pie with one hand and drink a beer with the other."

"Right." Ethan continued to use his knife and fork.

"Maybe people from San Fran don't like to eat with their hands," I said.

Ethan grimaced. His attention turned to me. "San Francisco. It's called San Francisco."

I swallowed. "Sorry. I just thought it was shortened to San Fran."

"Only outsiders call it that."

Noted. I didn't want to insult anyone else by calling it San Fran. It seemed like a touchy subject.

Bailey raised his eyebrows. "So you don't shorten it at all?"

"Some people shorten it to SF."

"SF," Rose repeated. "SF. San Fran." She cocked her head. "San Fran is easier to say."

Ethan didn't reply. He continued eating his pie with his knife and fork. Rose ate with gusto, licking the thick meat and gravy eagerly from her lips and then her fingers. She studied her plate, then poked at her veggies and mash with her fork. Her mouth twisted. There was likely a debate going on in her head about which to eat first.

"Do you like veggies, Ethan?" Rose asked.

"Yes."

For a teacher, he was very short on words. Rose's insistent stare pushed him for more of an answer.

"I love them now. As a kid, not so much."

"I don't know whether I'll like them when I'm old."

A smile tugged at the edge of Ethan's lips. Nice to see he had a sense of humour. He'd shown none of it up to now. Or a personality, even. I paused. That was harsh. The poor man had arrived and found out he'd have to share a house with us. It would take him some time to adjust.

Rose chose to eat her vegetables before her mash, picking at them slowly while studying Ethan. "Do you have a favourite vegetable?"

It seemed like Ethan wasn't going to get any peace. It was typical Rose style. She gave everyone an earbashing.

"Carrots," he said.

Rose grinned at him across the table. "Me too. Jack and Lily said that carrots help your eyesight. That's an even better reason to eat them. I wonder if mermaids eat carrots to help them see underwater."

Ethan cocked his head but didn't say anything.

Bailey continued to eat in silence. Every time someone spoke, he turned his face towards them and listened. But he never added to the conversation like he normally would with Rose and me. This was one of the reasons I was hesitant about having a relationship. I didn't want my children to feel uncomfortable or left out.

And I knew what men were like. They never wanted to be second fiddle. Even their own father wanted me to put him before our children. Granted, Max was probably at the extreme end of the scale when it came to thinking he was more important than anyone else. But still, I'd moved on from that shit. The children had men in their lives they could trust. Jack was a good role model—kind, and hardworking. And Ken, before he'd retired from being a ranger, had been a big part of their life. That was all they needed. That was all *I* needed.

Rose placed her knife and fork on the plate with a clink. She addressed Ethan. "Next Sunday we can have your favourite meal."

Next Sunday? How many Sundays until his house was finished and we'd have our home back? I hoped dinners became easier before then. *Hoped.* Maybe we could learn something more about the elusive Ethan as well. We'd just shared an entire meal with him and all I knew was that he liked carrots. And that didn't tell me much, except maybe he had good eyesight. At the very least, he had good eyes. I was trapped in them even when he was chastising me for my San Fran comment.

Let's hope he wasn't living with us long enough for me to insult him again. Or for me to be trapped in those hazel eyes again.

CHAPTER SIX

Ethan

WHEN I ENTERED the open-plan living area the next morning, Jasmine stood at the kitchen sink washing the dishes. It was 7am, and apparently, they'd already eaten breakfast. The children were in their bedroom, and from the snippets of conversation I heard drifting up the hallway, Bailey wanted to get dressed but Rose was annoying him.

I'd tried not to linger or eavesdrop on their conversation. Was this what most mornings were like? All cosy and familial? Everything I'd seen so far showed they connected as a family; nothing like my own growing up.

Dinner had been strange last night. I hadn't intended on joining them, but what else was I going to do? Jasmine had cooked enough for all of us, and it stood to reason that we would share meals together. Rose had talked the whole way through. It saved us from awkward silences.

Seeing we were alone, I took the time to study my co-worker. She was wearing a long-sleeved shirt and work shorts, the same uniform that she'd given me the evening before. She'd explained that we should wear long pants for most outdoor activities. But for days when we were at the office or on the boat, shorts were acceptable. I'd remembered to put sunscreen on this morning, Jasmine's words about the sun being strong down here echoing in my head.

She was all business today. Her long hair was tied back, giving her a more controlled persona. Her movements were sharp and deliberate. Not flowing like they had been yesterday. I tore my attention away. I'd been staring for way longer than I should.

"Good morning," I said as I entered the kitchen.

Jasmine gave me a smile. "Good morning. How did you sleep?"

"Good. The sound of the water lapping at the sand was like a lullaby."

She turned back to her task. Her calf muscles flexed as she reached for a plate on the counter. Why was I still watching her?

"The keys to the office are on the table. I need to drop the kids off at the school bus and then I'll meet you there."

As if on cue, Bailey came into the living room, Rose trailing behind. "Just leave him alone, Rose."

"He's my cat too. And if I want to make sure he's comfy, I will."

"Not having to listen to you all day will make him comfy," Bailey said.

"So will not having to smell you all day," Rose retorted.

They were both in the living room now. Neither acknowledged my presence.

Jasmine dried her hands on the towel. "Have you got everything?"

"Yes," they said.

"Go wait outside."

"Bye, Ethan." Rose waved as she rushed out the door.

Bailey looked at me and said a hasty, "Bye," before following his sister. They ran and jumped off the steps with more energy than anyone should have that early in the morning.

Jasmine picked up her keys and bag. "I'll get to the office around eight." She headed to the door, stopped mid-stride, and turned back to me. "Timmy has already been fed. Don't believe his 'I'm starving' act. And ignore his pleas to go outside. He's only allowed out under supervision."

"OK." That's all I managed to get out before she disappeared out the front door. It seemed like their mornings ran like clockwork. In my brother's house, mornings could be like mutiny on the high seas.

I acquainted myself with the kitchen and the lack of a coffee machine. Who could survive in this world without a good coffee in the morning? Jasmine apparently. For me, it was the smell of fresh coffee that awakened the senses. Hopefully, there was a machine at the office.

I popped some bread in the toaster and went to grab my phone. Only one bar of service. This place was remoter than remote, far beyond the black stump the guy had spoken about yesterday. I don't think half the people I knew could survive with no phone service. It didn't matter to me. Jasmine had told me they had good internet. That's all I needed for my research.

I connected to the internet to call my brother. Steve's face appeared on the screen. "Hey, Ethan. How's the land down under treating you?"

I set the phone down on the bench and buttered my toast. "I've been thrown a bit of a curve ball. The house I was meant to move into is being renovated." I grabbed my plate and phone and went out onto the porch. "I'm living with the female ranger and her kids."

Steve's eyes widened. "How many kids?"

"Two. A boy and girl." I took a bite of my toast.

Steve's lips turned upwards, and then he laughed. "Let the fun begin."

It was alright for him. He embraced his life which was often in disarray because of his mutinous crew. Especially since he often led the mutiny. I'd witnessed it on more than one occasion from my studio apartment above his garage. I was smart enough to just watch and not be convinced by my niece and nephew to join in their shenanigans.

"What about the female ranger? What's she like?"

"She's nice. Friendly. A bit awkward."

He nodded. "Having a stranger live with you would do that."

I wasn't helping on the awkward front. I was lucky she hadn't noticed how my eyes kept gravitating to her this morning. Imagine how awkward *that* would have been.

"And Haven Bay?"

I turned the camera around. "The view is magnificent."

"Fuck yeah. That alone is worth having to share your space."

"I don't think sharing my space is going to be conducive to finishing my dissertation. The kids are pretty loud and active."

He nodded. He worked from home when the kids were on vacation and was never as productive then. "Hopefully, your house will be renovated quickly."

I told him about the town as I ate my breakfast.

He shook his head. "I don't know how people live like that."

"I'll soon find out. I've got six months of it to look

forward to." I finished my toast and headed inside. "First day of work today. I can't wait to get out there and check out the sea lions."

"At the end of six months, this will all be worth it," he said.

Best I grab onto that optimism of his. Because this remote town, child roommates and a beautiful stranger in the kitchen every morning, might make me wonder if this was the best place to complete my dissertation.

JASMINE WALKED through the office door and zeroed in on me. The office was a portable building big enough for two desks, a wall of national park maps and leaflets, a fridge and a couple of extra chairs. No coffee machine.

She headed to her desk and turned her computer on. "During tourist season, we usually have a sea lion tour at 9.30 and if there's enough bookings, another one at 1."

I looked at my watch. Just over an hour until the next tour. I smiled. I was going to meet the sea lions, finally.

"There are no tours booked in this morning, so you can get started on your online inductions. And we'll need a copy of your car licence and boat licence to add to your file."

My stomach dropped. "Are we going out to see the sea lions today?"

"If you get your inductions done. And we need to check campers have paid their fees, clean the amenities at the campground, and refill brochures there and at the entries to the driving tracks close by."

I shifted in my seat. "I was hoping to see the sea lion colony to get an idea on how to structure my study."

Jasmine sighed and turned her chair to face me. "Your

job here is part-time ranger. The part-time part means that you have time to do your research. The part-time part comes first. It's what pays you, gives you a house to live in, a car to drive and a boat for your research."

I stiffened. There was nothing like being chastised by your new co-worker. She had that don't mess with me tone that mothers across the world had mastered. And she'd used it on me...a grown man.

I wasn't going to argue. What would I say anyway? I'd grown up learning quickly that it was not in my best interests to say anything. And when I got older, I never trusted myself not to be like my father. It would always be about who he could beat down with his words. And if necessary, his fists. I never wanted to be in a situation where I lost control like that, so I just shut up and put up.

And I doubt arguing would have a positive effect on Jasmine. She seemed to have a no-nonsense attitude, and I didn't want to get on her bad side seeing we had to live and work together. I needed that to be harmonious if my work and research were to be productive.

Jasmine stood. "I'm going to clean the campground, then I'll collect the mail."

I nodded and continued to work on my inductions. Jasmine stormed out of the office. Those long tanned legs sure could move fast.

Great. How was I supposed to work and live with her? Considering my words more than usual would be a good start.

CHAPTER SEVEN

Jasmine

"THAT MAN IS IMPOSSIBLE," I said to Lily and Jack. "When I told him he had an actual job to do and that his precious sea lions would have to wait, he was so fucking dismissive. He didn't even bother to respond."

I paced the floor in front of the counter while they shared a look. "And I have to live with him. He may look like sex on legs. But fuck me. He hardly says a word. I think he's smiled once since I met him."

Jack closed his newspaper, folded it and laid it flat on the counter. I wasn't ready for him to be all reasonable.

I ploughed on. "Who would want to live with someone like that? The sooner his house is renovated, the better."

Jack smoothed down the paper. "Now let's back up a bit."

Lily gave him a nudge. "To the sex on legs part?"

I rolled my eyes.

"Perhaps he didn't respond to your putting him in his place because he didn't want to have an argument," Jack said. "You know, because you have to work and live together."

Lily nodded. "Did you use your mum voice on him?"

"I used the voice that was necessary."

Lily laughed. "And you seriously thought that poor man would be brave enough to speak against it?"

"Poor man, nothing."

"Yes, poor man," Jack said. "He's moved halfway around the world to follow his passion to find out he needs to live with you, Bailey and Rose. Do you think that might have been a bit of a shock?"

I shrugged.

"Can we get back to the sex on legs part?" Lily asked, coming around the counter. "Did you get a good look at him, like maybe in a towel after a shower?"

I took a step back. "No."

Lily shadowed my move. "But you wanted to."

An image of Ethan in his wetsuit, torso bared, flashed through my mind. I blushed. "No."

She followed me to the door. I waved at Jack before she could ask another question. "Thanks for the chat."

"Put the poor man out of his misery and take him out to the sea lions," he said as the door closed behind me.

I supposed I should. It was cruel to deny him something so simple. I didn't even know why it had irked me so much. I don't know why *he* irked me so much. He hadn't been unpleasant to me or the children. And Rose could be full-on. Being quiet didn't equate to being rude. Not everyone was talkative.

Maybe he reminded me a bit of Max and how he'd always shirked his responsibilities. He always wanted to do the fun stuff, but none of the hard work to get there. Everyone else had to do the work, mainly me. Now, I only had to look after myself and Bailey and Rose. I didn't need to wait on someone else. I put *our* needs first.

That didn't give me permission to be rude or lack empathy. My thoughts and emotions were swirling around like they were in a whirlpool. I needed to control them. I needed to think of him like any other co-worker and show him the respect he deserved.

And I needed the same from him. The workload was too much for one person; he needed to do his part, so it didn't crush me.

As I made my way up the stairs, I could see Ethan through the door, bending down, picking up brochures. My eyes strayed to his butt. He looked much better in work shorts than Ken had. I drew a breath in. He was my co-worker. Those thoughts were not allowed.

CHAPTER EIGHT

Ethan

I SPUN around as Jasmine walked into the office and examined the floor strewn with maps and brochures. I couldn't pick them up fast enough.

"Did you open all the windows?" she asked.

"Yeah, I thought some fresh air would be nice."

"The window in the corner, where all the maps and brochures are, was the problem." She closed it, stopping the offending draught in an instant.

"Got it."

She knelt and started picking up the maps. "I'll sort all these out if you like. How are your inductions going?" Her tone was light.

Relief flooded through me. I didn't want to have angst between us. Not here or at home.

I went back to my desk. "Thanks. I got a couple of modules done."

She started laying the papers on the desk, sorting them

into piles. "Once I finish here, we can go out in the boat if you like."

"Yes, please."

What had changed? Did she realise how important it was to me? My ex-wife Audrey had never cared for my work. She once told me it bored her to tears. She'd even said that about me. Apparently, our relationship lacked passion. I'd done everything I could to make her happy. Knowing everything my mother had gone through, I'd tried to be the opposite of my father. Apparently, it wasn't enough. After six years of marriage, she left.

Jasmine finished sorting and started returning the maps and brochures to their allotted space.

"I've emailed you a copy of my licences," I said, to her back, not letting my eyes stray to those long legs as she reached up to reach the top holders.

When she'd finished her task, she returned to her computer and opened the email. "Your international car licence is good. But you can't drive a boat here on that licence."

I sucked a breath in. "What?"

"You'll need to get an Australian boat licence. You can't drive a boat until then."

"How long will that take?"

"The closest licence department is two hours away." She clicked some buttons and studied the screen. Typed a bit more. "The earliest appointment is in a month's time."

My stomach dropped. "What about my research?"

Jasmine shook her head. "I don't know. We'll try to work something out." She entered some details into the computer. "You're all booked in."

I didn't want to sit idle for one month. I couldn't. There was so much I wanted to do, to learn. I was going to be at her mercy. No, that wasn't correct. The job's mercy. There was enough work here for her and a part-timer. That's why I'd been hired. I couldn't expect her to take time out of her day, every day, to help me. Maybe she could manage if it was only one month. So far, nothing about this expedition had gone to plan.

I continued on my inductions until Jasmine said, "Are you ready to head out? If we go now, we should be back in time for a late lunch."

"I'm ready." I gave her a smile and stood up. I grabbed the waterproof satchel that held my tablet and note pads. Jasmine followed me out and locked the door behind us. She changed the time on the board, letting people know we'd be back at 1 pm. Two hours from now. Was that going to be enough time?

She led me out onto a small jetty straight in front of the general store with the National Park boat tied to it. I'd say it was a fifteen-seater. Nice and big for tours and snorkelling equipment. She undid the ropes and invited me to hop on. I watched as she went through the safety checks. The person I'd met yesterday seemed to have disappeared and been replaced by this efficient, precise person.

She started the boat, and I sat in the co-pilot chair beside her.

"How far is the sea lion colony?" I asked.

"Fifteen minutes from here. Because we're in a bay it's usually an easy, smooth ride."

The beach and houses receded. Ahead of us stretched clear blue water. I sighed. This place was paradise—secluded, untouched, unpolluted. Perfect for sea lions.

"How big is your colony here?"

Jasmine glanced at me before moving her attention back

to the water. "I'd estimate around 400. When I first started nearly five years ago, there were more."

Sea lion population decline was typical around the world. They were listed as endangered. Hopefully, some of the work I was doing would help change that. My PhD had been years in the making. A bachelor's degree, a master's degree, teaching assistant, research, and experience would all lead to my doctorate and helping sea lions.

"The data I collect will help with more accurate figures."

Jasmine frowned. "I'm sure our figures are close. We take counts every month."

I kept my mouth shut. I hadn't meant to insinuate their methods were inferior. In research circles, data was king. We didn't just rely on visual counts. I concentrated on the peace around us and the sea breeze against my skin rather than the silence in the boat.

"I won't only be collecting data on the size of the population. It will cover the demographics as well." I hoped that would help her understand my previous comment better.

Jasmine nodded. I didn't know if that meant she was interested or not. I continued, "I'll investigate their territory, interactions, everything. I can help determine why their numbers are declining. It will help develop policies for the future."

"How do you propose to collect this data?" Jasmine asked as she slowed the boat.

"I'll tag all the sea lions and place satellite trackers on some."

The boat rounded a point into a secluded area. Sea lions lay on the beach and rocks, sunning themselves. My heart quickened. I couldn't take in the scene in front of me fast enough. My eyes darted from group to group.

These beautiful creatures had once been hunted for their fur; their numbers were decimated. Then came gillnet fishing, causing sea lions to drown after being caught in the mesh. The South Australian government, which Jasmine and I worked for, banned gillnet fishing close to colonies and had cameras installed on all fishing boats so that deaths were accurately recorded. Deaths were reduced by 98%. Their actions were exactly why I'd approached them about funding my research.

I studied the sea lions in front of me. The males stood out, being twice the size of the females and having much darker fur. Juveniles were scattered across the sand, oblivious to the world. The sea lions barely paid us any attention, only glancing at us before returning to their slumber. Interesting.

It would take at least a month to tag them all and collect data on the individuals, and I'd need Jasmine's help to do it. How were we going to make this work? We had differing priorities. The research I was completing was not just about my dissertation, it was for the benefit of sea lions across the world.

CHAPTER NINE

Jasmine

I watched Ethan's reaction as his gaze raced across the scene in front of us. His head jerked as he looked from one spot to the next. A small smile stretched into a large one. My stomach lifted as he transformed in front of me. His hands had a slight shake, almost as if his excitement was trying to escape.

His sigh seemed to reset him. He lost the shakes, and his eyes stopped flitting from group to group. He turned to me. "You bring tourists here?"

"Yes, most days during tourist season."

"And what do the tourists do? How close do they get?" His eyes were piercing.

Again with the accusations? I stood tall. "You claim to like your research. Didn't you do any about us?"

He looked away. Disengaging again. Well, not me. If he was going to accuse me of something, he better be ready to hear my response. My days of being reticent were over.

"When we arrive, we give the tourists some information about the sea lions. We reiterate that the sea lions are wild animals. It is up to them if they approach or not. We don't feed or entice them." I gave Ethan a hard stare. "The guests then hop into the water. We remind them that the sea lions are fun and curious. If they are approached by one, they should interact." I watched as a young sea lion concentrated on us from the shore, its wide eyes staring. "The sea lions play and swim for as long as they want to. The guide watches everything closely." I glanced toward the shore. The sea lion walked to the water's edge, still watching us. "The swimmers learn about sea lions, get close and personal, and leave with a greater appreciation for them."

Ethan nodded.

"Is that enough information for you?"

"Yes." His reply held no sarcasm, unlike mine.

Who did he think he was, questioning my integrity, questioning whether I was looking after the sea lions' best interests? I had pulled more than one swimmer out of the water when I didn't like their attitude or actions.

"We will need to come out every day to do the tagging," he said.

I clenched my fists. I almost wanted to strangle him.

"I, *we*, have thousands of hectares to look after. There are multiple campgrounds within the park that need to be checked and maintained. Coming into summer, we need to ensure the fire trails are clear. We answer queries via email and phone daily. There are tours we need to conduct." I let all that sink in. "I will bring you when I can."

He nodded, continuing to watch the sea lions. The face he presented to them was different to the one he presented to me. It was enthusiastic and alive. I guess I deserved some of it seeing I'd been abrupt. But I had also tried to be welcoming. He needed to meet me halfway.

I'd already thought about the predicament we were in when he'd mentioned tagging. His lack of boat licence meant I'd need to bring him out every day. I'd been doing this job on my own for three months since Ken had retired. I hadn't had a day off since then. There were so many jobs to do here that I needed a full-time ranger, not a part-time one. And certainly not a part-time ranger whose mind lay elsewhere. And now it looked like I would be part-time too, seeing head office insisted I support him as much as I could. How was I going to make it work? And not neglect my children!

His comment about coming out every day had sent me over the edge. I don't know if it was because he was presumptuous or because he made me feel like this was more important. Whatever it was, it hit the wrong button. And for the second time that day, I'd let him have it.

Water splashed against the boat. Ethan was leaning over the side. His grin was back. The juvenile sea lion that had been watching us was doing tumble turns. I went to the rear of the boat and walked down the steps until I could reach the water. I swished my hand around, making splashing sounds. Within moments, the sea lion was beside me, bobbing up and down. Ethan was watching us.

"Bang on the side of the boat, see if he comes back to you," I said.

Ethan followed my instruction. The sea lion was there in an instant. Ethan chuckled—a deep, smooth sound that made me feel like I was floating. Gosh, that sound could be addictive. I shook my head. I would not get addicted to the sound or anything about Ethan. Except maybe the need for him to move into his own home. I was already addicted to that idea.

I splashed the water again. The sea lion flashed toward me, then flung itself in another direction.

Ethan's study was important. The tagging was important. How was I going to make this work?

CHAPTER TEN

Ethan

I LET the warm sun and gentle breeze calm my mixed emotions as I made my way to the store. Small waves brought the tide higher. Their constant rhythm was soothing, telling me that the world remained mostly unchanged. Just my world was a little different.

I'd finished my first ranger shift. It had been a mixture of emotions, ranging from tense to joyous. Jasmine was still working, probably relieved to have some time to herself.

The bell rang as I entered the store. Jack greeted me. "How's it going today, Ethan? Did Jasmine take you out to see the sea lions?"

I slowed and approached the counter. I wasn't intending to make this a social visit. All I needed was milk. "Yes. They're closer than I expected."

Jack closed his book. "What sort of research are you going to do?"

"I need to tag them. Then there will be a lot of monitoring and data collection. I'll study their interactions, where they feed, the quality of the water, their movements and relationships."

Jack's eyes widened. "That's a lot of info." He reached under the counter and pulled out two beers. "Would you like one?"

"Yes, please."

After the day I'd had, I wasn't going to say no. So much for not making this a social call. Jasmine had swayed from approachable to antagonistic all day. I'd tried to stay calm and not do anything to annoy her. But my existence alone probably did that. I needed to remember three things—I'd be moving into my own home soon, what I was doing was for my career and the sea lions, and I'd only be here for six months.

"Let's sit on the porch and enjoy the view."

I followed him out and sat on a chair beside him. "So you'll be going out most days to observe and collect data then?"

My mouth twisted. "When Jasmine has time. It appears my boat licence isn't valid here."

"Oh." Jack looked down at his hands and back to the sandy beach. "That's going to be tough. She's been working seven days a week for three months straight. She's exhausted."

My grip tightened on my beer. That explained her reaction. She would have thought I was here to help, not create more work for her. Everything I did created more work. Her having to rearrange her house, her having to teach me about the job even though I was only here for a short time, and now she had to join me on my research trips.

"Did the other ranger work part-time?"

"It was a flexible arrangement. He worked more hours when Jasmine needed him and less hours when she didn't."

I nodded. The more hours part would be now that tourist season had started. And here I was, taking those hours away from her.

"Jasmine will make it work," Jack assured me. "She always does."

I rubbed my hand over my face. I hadn't thought of Jasmine or my part-time role enough. I'd concentrated solely on how everything would affect my research. She must have thought I was a selfish ass.

Laughter carried on the wind. Bailey and Rose were playing with the kitten in the sand again. Jasmine had picked them up half an hour ago. I hadn't added them into the equation either. I needed to lift my game.

This is exactly how my father would have behaved, thinking what he wanted was of greatest important. He'd never considered anyone else. We'd suffered repeatedly because of his selfishness. Like the time he wanted to go to a big football game with friends. He had to get the best seats, which meant we didn't have enough money for food the next week. And somehow that was our fault because we ate too much.

"The kids would love to help you," Jack said. "Bailey especially. He's into everything nature. Rose... she's happy to do anything Bailey's doing."

I shifted in my seat. I wasn't so sure about that. Bailey had hardly spoken to me since I'd arrived. Rose made up for him though. Maybe he was shy. Besides that, they didn't seem to stay still for long. Would they be able to stop and listen to instructions? Or would they just be a distraction? I was leaning towards the latter.

I looked at the children. "I'll speak to Jasmine so we can figure out how to make it work, include the kids, if that suits her best."

"Good plan. Tell me more about the research."

We sat and spoke for the next hour until Jasmine collected the children on her way home. She glanced at us as she walked past, offering a wave, but nothing more. Her attention was on the children and collecting the kitten she then carried in her arms. This was her softer side. The side that wasn't annoyed at me. I much preferred this side.

I stood up. "Best I grab the milk I came for and go. Jasmine might need my help."

Jack smiled and held his hand out for my empty bottle. Was he smiling at the stupidity of my statement? I doubted Jasmine needed my help with anything. I wondered how long she'd been single for. She seemed to have her shit together at home and at work. That made me think it had been a while.

Even though towards the end of our marriage, Audrey and I were living separate lives, it had still taken a while for me to adjust to my new single life. I'd had to become responsible for everything. There was no sharing the load. That was hard enough. Imagine if there were children as well.

Mothers were amazing in all they did. Single mothers even more so. From what I'd seen, Jasmine was a great mom and had an excellent work ethic. The way she balanced both was a testament to her strong will and being able to speak her mind. My mother had neither of those.

I could say I had one of those traits at least; my strong will got Steve and me through our childhood. It would get me through these six months and help me be a better work partner for Jasmine.

CHAPTER ELEVEN

Jasmine

ETHAN and I were in the office. He was at his desk entering sea lion details into a database. We'd been out most days in the past two weeks tagging sea lions. We were probably halfway through them. With each sea lion we tagged, Ethan would record as much information as he could.

I stole glances at him while he concentrated. His brow furrowed as he checked his notes. After that, he stared steadily at the screen, typing. There were many faces to Ethan Shaw. Some were more secretive than others, like the small smile when Rose said something snarky to Bailey and he replied with perfect understated sarcasm. Or the way he tried to hide his annoyance when the kids interrupted his report writing in his room. I had to give him credit. He was never rude or nasty to them.

The phone rang. I hoped it was the cabinet maker. He'd been saying for two weeks that he had nearly finished the kitchen and would be out soon to put it in. It was November now and if I didn't keep on top of them, the house wouldn't be finished by the Christmas break. And Ethan would still be living with us.

"Hello, Jasmine speaking."

"Hi, Jasmine, it's Paul the tiler."

"Hi, Paul. I haven't heard from the cabinet maker today."

"He better get a hurry on. I keep booking jobs in and at this rate I won't have any space left before Christmas."

I clenched the phone. Dealing with tradies was worse than dealing with young campers. "Please keep a week open for me. I'm going into town tomorrow. I'll hassle him in person."

"That's a good idea. That's my normal tactic with him. I'll slot you in for two weeks' time."

"Thanks," I said before I disconnected.

After the tiler would be the painter and the floor people. We were cutting it close. If it wasn't done before Christmas, we'd have to wait until halfway through January for them to start work again. I closed my eyes and took a deep breath. It could be worse. Ethan could be an arsehole.

The messenger app beeped. I looked at my phone at the same time Ethan looked at his. It was a message from Jack. *Ethan has a parcel.*

Ethan smiled. What was that all about? It would be nosey to ask. We weren't exactly friends. Or were we? If I lived with someone else, would I ask them? There went the whirlpool of thinking again. I'd had my life under control for five years and certainly hadn't overthought anything in the last four. This was ridiculous.

"What's in the parcel?"

Ethan smiled that damn charming smile of his. "It's a surprise. I'll show you when we get home."

Argh. I would be counting the hours down until we got

home to see what the parcel was. I didn't want him to see how curious I was, so I went back to work filling out the daily tour report. I looked at the time. Still an hour and a half to go before I left to pick up the kids. So still two hours in total before we got home, and I could see what was in the parcel.

ROSE AND BAILEY charged inside the house, dumping their things as they went. Seriously, every day it was the same. They stopped short at the kitchen counter where a big box sat.

"What's in the box?" Bailey asked Ethan.

"Something to make my mornings better."

That was cryptic. The only thing that would make my mornings better was for Rose and Bailey to stick to the routine. Maybe there were whips in there.

Did Sex on Legs like to use whips? I blushed. What the fuck was I thinking?

"Are you going to open it?" Rose asked, climbing up onto one of the chairs at the counter. She tucked her short hair behind her ears. It had been short since she was four and had declared that long hair was annoying.

Ethan nodded and got a knife out of the drawer. He sliced along the tape and lifted the flaps. Then he reached inside and pulled out another box. I tried not to notice how his biceps flexed as he was lifting it out. Trying and doing were two different things. I was only human.

"A coffee maker?" Bailey asked.

That's all he needed to make his mornings better?

"There's nothing better than the smell of fresh coffee to awaken your senses," Ethan said.

Rose stared at him. "Where are you going to put it?"

"I was hoping your mom would let me have some counter space?" He looked over at me, raising his eyebrows and giving me a smile.

I shrugged. "Sure."

Bench space was easier than storing whips. I held my laughter in. As much as I hated to say it, this was Ethan's home too. And I needed to be accommodating for at least another few weeks.

"How does it work? Are you going to make one now?" Bailey asked.

"It might be too late in the day for your mom."

"No, it's fine," I said.

"I bought one that can make coffee as well as hot chocolate for you and Rose."

Rose clapped her hands. Bailey grinned. That was very thoughtful of Ethan. He didn't need to consider the children in his decision-making. Max never would have, and he was their own father.

"How about I set the machine up while you put your stuff away?" he said to the children.

Rose jumped off the seat, grabbed her schoolbag and placed it next to her bookshelf, where it belonged. Then she placed her school shoes next to it. She ran to her room and was back in no time, putting her school uniform in the wash. Bailey hadn't budged. He was watching Ethan unpack the box.

"Bails, put your stuff away or else we won't get hot chocolate," Rose said.

Ethan twisted his mouth like he was trying not to laugh at Rose's insistence. He caught my eye and his lips quirked.

I sidled up to him and whispered, "Hot chocolate might be my new reward system if they do their chores."

Bailey reluctantly turned away and did as his sister said. I kept myself busy unpacking their lunch boxes. It had been a long time since I'd had anything but instant coffee. There were no coffee shops in Haven Bay and I was usually too busy when we went to Somewhere Bay to stop for one. Could it be as good as Ethan said?

Rose watched Ethan. "What are you doing now?"

"I've put the water in and now I'm putting the milk in. It goes in this plastic part at the back. When we're finished making the coffee or hot chocolate, we can pull it off and put it in the fridge to keep the milk fresh."

That was a good idea. I liked the idea of not wasting the milk.

Ethan pulled two packets out of the box. One was hot chocolate and the other was coffee. He reached in again and pulled out some glass cups with lids. "These cups are reusable. Not like what they use in coffee shops, so we won't be adding to waste."

Bailey sat down at the bench. "Have you seen that TV show *War on Waste*?"

Ethan shook his head.

"You should see how many coffee cups are thrown away every day. And they can't be recycled because they have plastic lining. Australians use one billion coffee cups a year."

Ethan turned to Bailey, considering him, and then gave him a small smile. I was watching the moment a connection was formed.

"A lot of cups end up in the ocean." Ethan said. "After a long time, they break down into small pieces and marine life thinks it's food."

Rose's eyes became big circles. "Do they eat it?"

Ethan nodded. "Yes. They can get very sick."

"And die?" she asked, her voice tentative.

"Yes," Ethan said.

I appreciated that he didn't sugarcoat it. The children needed to know that humans were responsible for environmental damage.

"This machine doesn't use coffee pods," Ethan said. He looked at Bailey. "So even less waste goes into a landfill."

Bailey smiled. I smiled too at my little environmentalist.

I stood by Ethan as he made them a hot chocolate. He pointed to a button. "This button is for warm rather than scorching hot. It will be safe for the kids to drink straight away."

This coffee machine may have been his indulgence, but he'd made sure it was suitable for all of us. He set to the coffee next. He was right. The scent was amazing, all earthy and smoky and just glorious as I breathed it in. Calmness spread through me.

I was standing so close to Ethan I could feel his heat and smell him too. Salt and freshness direct from the ocean with a hint of something else, woody or musk maybe. I leant a little closer. God, he smelled good. It was a smell that drew you in. It had nothing to do with his smile or looks, but more to do with pure manliness. I jerked away. What the hell was I thinking?

Ethan looked at me, his head tilted. My face was burning. I reached for the coffee bag to read the ingredients and take my mind off him. I didn't know how that was ever going to work. The association between coffee and his manly smell would remain forever.

I needed to get over these thoughts. He might be kind and thoughtful, but it didn't mean anything. Maybe he was buttering me up because he needed my help. I could tell myself that, but I didn't really believe it.

CHAPTER TWELVE

Ethan

WE WALKED along the beach to the bonfire set up across the road from the shop.

Jasmine gave me a nudge and a grin. "Are you ready for your first small-town bonfire?"

"How's it different from a normal bonfire?"

"You'll see."

Her smirk had me worried. I turned my attention back to the people seated around the fire. I recognised Sara from the café, and Jack and Lily. There were two other men sitting amongst the circle. I assumed they were Ross and Jay.

Rose grabbed my hand and pulled me toward the seated group. I never had time to be nervous with her around.

"Everyone, this is Ethan. He's living with us. He works with Mum."

Everyone's eyes turned toward me.

"Hi." I shoved my hands in my pockets. I'd rather be studying sea lions than be the one being studied.

Rose dragged me over to Sara. "Miss Sara works at our school. She's the best teacher we have."

Sara laughed. "You don't think that when I give you assignments."

"That's because they're never about mermaids."

"That's what creative writing is for."

Rose rolled her eyes. She turned us to the two men next. "This is Ross and Jay."

They both stood up to shake my hand. Ross had wild curly hair and Jay short brown hair. They were the opposite of what I would've imagined.

"If you're ever sick, Ross will fix you in a jiffy. Last year I was vomiting and vomiting. He gave me this thing that stopped it."

Ross ruffled her hair. "It's called a wafer."

"Yeah. That."

Jay was smiling. "Jack tells me you're doing research on the sea lions."

There was that small-town thing again.

Bailey came over and stood beside me. "He's going to write a report that's going to help save them all over the world."

They were unexpected words. I hoped they were true.

"I hope to help guide policies to ensure their future."

Jay grinned. "I'm not sure how you get much work done with these two." He pulled Rose into his lap and tickled her. She squealed in delight.

"I try to give him some peace in the evenings," Jasmine said. "While I finish off paperwork, the kids do their home-work and Ethan works on his dissertation. Then I send the kids off for some quiet time."

Rose giggled. "Sometimes we're not very quiet though. Mum uses her mum voice on us."

I chuckled. It happened just about every night.

"Are you laughing because she uses the mum voice on you too?" Sara asked.

Everyone's eyes turned to me, including Jasmine's. I shifted my feet. She'd used it more than once.

Jasmine raised her eyebrows. I shrugged, returning her smirk from earlier.

Jack joined in. "She used it on him the first day at work. All that poor man wanted to do was go out to see the sea lions. All she wanted him to do was his boring inductions."

Jay shook his head at Jasmine. "So cruel."

She clenched her jaw. "Inductions are important."

"I helped her see the error of her ways," Jack said.

That explained her changed attitude when she came back from the shop.

Jasmine crossed her arms. "I would have taken him on my own."

Jack laughed. "Sure you would have. When he'd finished every last bit of your requirements."

Jasmine turned around and set up her chair. It was unlike her to disengage. That was my job.

Rose took my chair from me and set it up next to Jasmine's and then hers beside me. I listened to the banter back and forth. Lily was unusually quiet. She spent a lot of time looking between Jasmine and me with a little smile on her face.

"How's the coffee machine going?" Jack asked.

"Great. It's just what I need in the morning."

"Does the coffee smell good, Jasmine?" Lily asked.

"Yes," she answered curtly. She gave Lily a pointed look.

Lily laughed to herself and sat back in her chair. Jasmine huffed. Because of the smell of coffee?

More people arrived and the conversation changed to general chit-chat. Sara went off to cook the fish and chips. She'd bring out a few parcels at a time and hand them out. When she handed me a parcel, I tore the paper open. I wanted to taste the *best* fish and chips. I bit into some fish. Saltiness and sweetness spread across my taste buds. The fish melted in my mouth. Not bad at all. The chips were perfectly cooked. They weren't uniform in shape, which made me think they were homemade. I'd have to compliment the chef later.

Rose and Bailey studied me while I took my first few bites.

"It's hella good," I said.

Rose cocked her head. "Is that a word you use in San Francisco?"

I nodded.

The crowd dwindled after dinner, but the townspeople stayed behind. Rose sat on Jay's lap, yawning before resting her head. He rubbed her back as she fell asleep. Ross shared a look with him, both were smiling and content. I had a feeling that any child they had would be loved beyond measure.

"You two are making me all maternal," Sara said as she loosened her blonde plait.

"Says the woman who doesn't want children," Jay said.

"I don't need children when I'll have yours to share."

"Not everyone wants to have children," Jack said. "Some people act like it's defying the world order not to have them."

"What about you, Ethan? Do you have children waiting for you at home?" Lily asked.

I shifted in my seat. I hated this topic, especially when it came to my lack of parenting. While I was married, people would ask when Audrey and I would be having children. But like Jack said, there was no crime in not having children. And given my past, it was best not to.

So, while I'd rather run away than face the question, I answered instead. "No. Children were never in the cards for me and my ex-wife."

"How long were you married for?"

Another question I wasn't too fond of.

"Six years."

"Ross and Jay have been married for six years," Jasmine said.

Thank goodness. A change in topic. Jasmine had thrown me a lifeline. I gave her a smile and whispered a thank you to her.

She leant over. Her breath was warm against my skin. The warmth travelled through me. She whispered in my ear, "Welcome to small-town life. You'll get used to it."

Would I? I doubt I could get used to it in six months.

"I can't wait for another six years," Jay said, breaking into our conversation.

"To another six years." Ross raised his beer to Jay.

"And many more after that." Jay clinked his beer with Ross's.

"Even if you are as bossy as Jasmine sometimes."

"A woman knows what she wants." Jay gave Jasmine a wink.

"Lily and I have been married for thirty-one years. We met when we were eighteen."

"We got married one month later," Lily said. "Everyone thought we were crazy. We showed them." She took Jack's hand. He gave hers a squeeze.

"I think we're doing well," Jasmine said to me. "We've survived a month."

"Because of the coffee," Lily said.

"I'd like to think it was because of our good advice," Jack said.

"You can think that if you like." Lily kissed his cheek.

These people were happy. Maybe there was something to this small-town life. They all shared openly, not fearing recrimination. They teased and taunted each other but not in a bitter way. I felt like they supported each other. I didn't have a circle of friends like this in San Francisco. The only people in my circle were my brother and grandparents.

The way Jasmine had saved me from their questions made me appreciate her even more. Audrey would have left me hanging. Like when people asked the baby question, she would always look pointedly at me, even though it was something we'd agreed on early in our marriage. Jasmine may have been terse at times, but she was a good person. If she wasn't, these people wouldn't love and respect her.

I was respected for my work and determination. I'm not sure that equated to being respected as a person though. I guess to be respected as a person, I'd need people to see who I really was. But I was too busy hiding from the world.

JASMINE and I headed to the tour meeting point. A few guests had gathered.

"I'd like to try something different with the wetsuits today if that's OK," I said. I didn't want her to think I was trying to take over. This was her world, and I was only in it for a short time.

"What do you have in mind?"

"Some guests seem to have difficulty in following the

wetsuit instructions. It was the same with some of my students. I found giving them a demonstration helped."

It also helped keep the distance between me and the students. Some of the females, although fully capable, would ask for help so they could get close to me. I'd begun to wonder if that's why they took my class. I don't know. Some students had crushes on their teachers. The wetsuit demonstration helped put an end to it because I often got the students to help each other.

"OK. There's no harm in trying."

We waited for everyone to arrive and then I grabbed my wetsuit and gave a demonstration on the easiest way to put it on. When I turned around to show the guests how to pull the wetsuit up, Jasmine was watching my every move, her mouth slightly agape. I paused for a second, heat rushing up my cheeks. My silence must have alerted her that something was wrong. Her eyes rose to my face and when she saw me looking at her, she blushed and her eyes darted away. She spun around and busied herself with checking her list.

I swallowed and got on with my demonstration. When I turned to Jasmine the second time, her eyes were on the guests. I breathed a sigh of relief.

The guests went off to get changed and I approached Jasmine, keeping my wetsuit zipped up tight.

"That seemed to go well," Jasmine said.

"No one's called for help yet so that's a good sign."

She nodded. "Your demonstration was good. Very thorough."

"You can give it a go next time."

"No thanks. I wouldn't feel comfortable parading myself like that. I don't have a body like yours." She blushed so deeply that if I'd touched her cheek, I'd probably burn my hand.

If she touched mine, she would feel the heat from my anger. I clenched my jaw. The word *parading* cut deep. "I don't do it to show off."

"I didn't mean that you do. I'm sorry." She sounded genuine, but she was the one who'd implied it. If she didn't mean it, then why did she say it?

Audrey had accused me of the same thing. Like I wanted the attention, when in fact I wanted the opposite. My father always wanted attention. I learned when I was young it was better to give it to him than draw it to myself.

I nodded and walked away.

She grabbed my arm. "I'm sorry, Ethan. My words were completely inappropriate."

I faced her but didn't make eye contact. "It's easier to show than explain. And it means the guests won't have to ask me for help." I shrugged. "Students often asked me. Trying to flirt. It made me uncomfortable."

"That was a smart way to combat the problem." She was trying hard to redeem herself.

"I thought so."

I walked back to the guests who were starting to emerge from the changing rooms. I needed to be far away from Jasmine at that moment. My stomach tightened every time I thought about what she'd said. *Parading*.

The way she'd compared my body to hers also stirred something inside me that shouldn't have been stirred. I'd noticed more than once her body's curves, her tanned legs and other things I shouldn't have noticed. I'd had to hold my tongue when she'd said her body was nothing like mine. Because if I hadn't, I would have told her that many a man would have enjoyed watching her put on a wetsuit. Including me.

CHAPTER THIRTEEN

Jasmine

ETHAN WAS AWAY, getting his boat licence at long last. The day was dragging on. I'd already cleaned the campgrounds, done the swimming tour and answered emails. I had some other campsites to clean in the National Park, so I'd hit that after I collected the mail.

Jack and Lily were on the porch, reading and soaking up the morning sun.

Lily looked up and gave me a cheeky smile. "Good morning. Enjoy the smell of coffee this morning?"

I rolled my eyes. "You're really not funny. I'm not going to tell you anything from now on. You obviously can't be trusted."

She gave a shrug. "I'm not the one who enjoys the smell of her housemate better than the smell of fresh coffee."

"You're impossible."

Jack laughed. He put his book on the side table.

"Where's Sex on Legs this morning?" Lily asked. "You two are usually joined at the hip."

I crossed my arms. "That's normally what happens when you're teaching someone."

"He told me last night he was going to get his licence today," Jack said.

"Do you miss him?" Lily's cheeky smile returned.

I wanted to slap her...figuratively, of course. "Not really. I've got plenty to do."

She smirked. "That's why you're here."

"I'm here to collect the mail. Is there any for us?"

"It's *us* now, is it?" Jack said.

"Well, it is the department's mail and we do work for the department."

"Uh-huh."

Neither of them made a move. I'd have to check myself. I uncrossed my arms and headed for the door.

"Quite a show Ethan put on yesterday," Lily said.

I stopped in my tracks and spun around. "What are you talking about?"

"The wetsuit demonstration. You couldn't take your eyes off him."

Jack gave her a nudge. "More like *you* couldn't take your eyes off him. You wouldn't leave the porch until it was over."

Lily shrugged. "Beautiful things should be admired."

"What about me?"

"You're beautiful in other ways."

I returned to my former spot and stared them down. "Ethan doesn't do the wetsuit demonstration for attention. It's practical."

Jack and Lily shared a look. My shoulders tensed.

"That's twice in the last two days you've stuck up for him," Jack remarked.

These two were impossible. Making things up where they didn't exist. "Now what are you talking about?"

"When we were asking him about having children and being married," Jack said.

"Not everyone is comfortable with small-town mentality where everyone knows everything."

"Weren't you at least curious?" Lily asked.

Of course, I was curious. I like to know people and what makes them tick. I'd like to know what makes Ethan tick. The most personal thing he'd mentioned since being here was that he didn't like it when students flirted with him. I'd been shocked at this revelation. Not because it was the opposite of Max who played on his looks, but because Ethan had been so offended by my misused words and he'd spoken up about it. He hardly ever spoke up about anything unless it had to do with the sea lions.

I had to admit I thought the demonstration was ridiculous at first. But that had to do more with me than the actual activity. And when he'd explained it, I understood. I had to admit to myself that I'd made a mistake in judging him. And the demonstration was effective. Most people had put their wetsuits on without assistance.

"Jasmine?" Lily prompted, bringing me back to the conversation.

What were we talking about? Whether I was curious about Ethan. "No, I wasn't curious."

Jack laughed his deep hearty laugh. "Now you're bull-shitting."

I walked away. "I'm going to get the mail."

What was it with these people? When Ethan took Rose from Jay to carry her home on the night of the bonfire, Jay had made sure to hold me back to tell me Ethan was a nice guy. I was pretty sure I could determine who was or wasn't nice on my own. And whether Ethan was nice or not didn't matter as long as he did his job. And treated the kids well. And didn't make me uncomfortable in my own home.

CHAPTER FOURTEEN

Ethan

I WALKED out into the kitchen at my usual time surprised to see the kids at the table eating their breakfast. Jasmine wasn't out yet. I could hear her moving at the other end of the house. It looked like this morning wasn't running to plan.

"Are your lunch boxes packed?" I asked.

Bailey shook his head. His short brown wavy hair was unbrushed. "No," he said around a mouthful of food.

I turned and looked at the counter. I could have answered that myself. They were sitting in their usual waiting place. The snacks were already in there. I grabbed their sandwich containers out of the fridge. Jasmine didn't use wasteful lunch wrap, another thing to admire about her. I got the juice boxes next, and ice packs out of the freezer and put them in the lunch box. Then I placed them in their school bags.

I looked at the time. They were running too far behind. I'd need to help with more than just the lunch box.

Jasmine arrived in the doorway wrapped in a towel, her tanned skin covered in droplets of water. They were sticking to her like they never wanted to leave. I'd be the same. The towel was tucked in at the top of her ample breasts and fell to the top of her thighs. My gaze flicked from top to bottom. For fuck's sake, I wasn't a horny teenager. I reluctantly moved my gaze to her face. Thank goodness she hadn't noticed me staring.

"Get your lunch ready, please," she said to Bailey and Rose.

"Ethan has already done it," Rose said.

She looked in my direction like she hadn't even noticed I'd been standing there. "Thanks."

"Go and get dressed," I said. "I'll sort these two."

She glanced down at her towel-clad body and blushed. A brisk turn and she was headed to her room. "Thanks," she called out.

No, *thank you*. That was the best thing I'd seen in many a morning.

Rose was taking her time chewing her toast, staring off into space.

"Rose, chew faster," I said. "Bailey, bring me your plate and go do your teeth."

He got up straight away.

"If you move quicker, you'll have more time in peace," I said, indicating to Rose. He almost ran to their room. "Rose, you have thirty seconds left."

She chewed fast and brought me her plate.

"You know the drill." I pointed her in the direction of their bathroom.

I put some toast in for Jasmine and started a coffee for her. It was unlike her to be late like this. In the nearly two months I'd lived with them, she'd never been late. I guess everyone got tired coming up to the end of the year. Even Jasmine, the super mom.

There was movement from the kids' room but that didn't mean anything. Either of them could get distracted as easily as the other. "I need you out here in thirty seconds to put your shoes on," I yelled out.

Jasmine rushed into the kitchen, tying her hair back. "Thanks for your help. My alarm didn't go off."

"The kids will be ready in a minute. Here's some toast and coffee for your drive."

"Thanks. I don't know what I would have done without you."

Bailey and Rose came in behind her, grabbed their shoes and put them on.

Rose glanced at me as she was tying her shoelaces. "You're as bossy as Mum."

"I learned from the best." I leaned a hip against the counter and crossed my arms with a grin. "How was my mom voice?"

"Terrifying," Rose said. That was a new word for her.

"I did a good job then."

Jasmine narrowed her eyes. "Terrifying, huh?"

"Well, you know..."

Jasmine smiled at me. My heart lifted.

I couldn't imagine two months ago that I'd be bantering with her like this. Friends do that, right?

"Go. I'll meet you at the office," I said.

She grabbed her keys and shuffled the kids out the door. It was nice to know I could help her for a change.

I NEEDED to get some milk before I headed home. The afternoon had been good. I'd driven the boat out for the first time. Jasmine had joined me even though I hadn't expected her to. She always had so much other work to do. But I'd enjoyed her company. The questions she'd asked had made me think on a deeper and more practical level, like asking why population growth was so slow. I would miss our trips together. But it would be selfish to expect Jasmine to continue coming out with me.

Jack was at the counter doing a crossword puzzle. He gave me a grin when I entered. "Saw you head out on the boat today."

"It was good to drive myself for a change." I went to grab a carton of milk.

"Jasmine went with you."

"Yeah." What was he getting at?

"Did she think you'd be lonely by yourself?"

"No, she just wanted to make sure I knew where I was going."

"Surely, after all your trips you would know where you're going."

I made my way back to the counter. I placed the carton of milk down and grabbed some coins from my pocket.

Lily was standing beside Jack, smiling. "Maybe she was going to be lonely without you."

While I would have liked to think that, I'm sure it wasn't the case. She always put safety first and that's what she had been doing this time.

"I doubt that." I put the coins on the counter.

"Maybe she thought she owed you one for helping her this morning," Jack said.

How did these people know everything that went on in town?

"She doesn't owe me. If anything, it's the other way around. She's helped me a lot since I've been here."

I wasn't trying to win brownie points. She needed help. That was it, plain and simple. It's not something I would remind her of when I needed something for myself. That's not how I operated.

"She seems to tolerate you more these days," Lily said.

"Like Jack tolerates you." I gave her a smirk.

"Oh, Jack tolerates me in a lot of ways." She returned my smirk. She knew she'd trumped me. I needed to be smarter at this game.

"I think we have gained a mutual respect," I said. "Hopefully that lasts until my house is ready to move into."

The sooner the better. Because getting too close to Jasmine and her children was risky. Thank goodness my assignment here was only six months.

"Thanks for the milk." I walked out quickly so I couldn't engage in any more of their small-town talk.

Why was I hoping Jasmine wanted to spend time with me? If anything, I should want her to spend less time with me. Forming some sort of relationship with her, Bailey and Rose was not my intention, but it was hard not to when we lived together. I didn't want to be rude and exclude myself. But at the same time, I didn't want to include myself.

The distance I thought I needed to keep was becoming shorter and shorter. I should try to make it the opposite. But could I?

CHAPTER FIFTEEN

Jasmine

Ethan stood up from his desk. "I've answered the emails I could. There were a couple of tricky ones though."

I smiled up at him. "Thanks. I'll do them before I head to the boat."

"I'll head out to the campground, do the cleaning and meet you there." He strode down the stairs, and I watched him until he was out of sight. I found myself watching him more and more. Since that first day two months ago, he'd become helpful at work and at home. He never complained if we had to put ranger duties before his research. It was a relief to have someone I could rely on.

He wouldn't be moving into the house next door before Christmas. The tiler would be finished in time, but not the painter or carpet layer. In a way, I would miss his presence when he left. But next door wasn't the other side of the world.

I answered the remaining emails and headed out to the boat. Our guests would start arriving soon and needed to be sized up for their wetsuits before going into the change rooms. Even though we were heading into summer, the water was still a little cold for swimming in normal swim gear.

Ethan arrived soon after and prepped his wetsuit. While I did a safety check of the boat, he separated the wetsuits into piles by size. As the guests arrived, we started handing them out.

Next came what I had begun to refer to as the best start to a tour, ever. Ethan stripped down to his bike shorts and guided the guests through the process of putting on a wetsuit. He started with his back to me, so I got to watch his butt and back muscles flex as he pulled the wetsuit up. When he got it to his waist, he turned to show everyone where it sat.

And that's when I got to stare at his broad shoulders that led down to a narrow waist, not like *He-Man*, better, real. Then there was his smooth chest. I licked my lips. Would it be rock hard or soft to the touch? What the hell was I even thinking? I did not want to touch Ethan.

I sighed. His body was better than in the photos. Tanned, toned, divine. It was better than a morning coffee. And that was saying something because I couldn't go without one in the morning, even if it was just an instant one like I had before the magic coffee machine arrived.

I forced myself to turn away. It was completely inappropriate for me to ogle my co-worker. It didn't stop the two twenty-somethings on the tour from doing the same. I clenched my teeth. After he finished his presentation, Ethan joined me. I'd stowed his tablet in the waterproof box beside the helm. As much as he wanted to, it was unlikely that he'd have time to do any work while on the tour. He always brought it anyway.

Ethan looked at the horizon. Dark grey clouds had formed. "Do you think the storm will hit us?"

"Yes, this afternoon sometime."

"Is there anything special we need to do to prepare?"

"We'll need to make sure there is no loose debris at the campground, put some storm safety signs up, make sure the campers are aware and secure, and check all the windows at the office and at home are shut tight."

"Easy. I'm sure we can do all that before it hits."

"I'll need to leave early to pick up the kids. I don't want to drive home from the bus stop in the middle of it."

Storms could be gnarly out here, the wind so strong it would push the car sideways and the rain so heavy you couldn't see through the windshield.

"I can do the other jobs while you get them."

My shoulders relaxed and I smiled up at him. I'd been concerned I wouldn't be able to fit it all in. I still couldn't bring myself to ask for help. Ethan probably wouldn't say no. But that wasn't the point. The children were my responsibility. No one else's. If someone offered help, like he just had, that was a different story.

"Excuse me, Ethan," one of the twenty-somethings said as she approached. "Can you zip my wetsuit up, please?"

I stepped forward with a fake sweet smile before Ethan had a chance to reply. "I'll do that for you."

Her face dropped but she turned around anyway. Me zipping her up was better for all of us. No mixed messages involved. And I knew Ethan hated the attention. When I finished, her friend joined her and they started talking to Ethan, giggling and flipping their long locks. Seriously, he was at least ten years older than them and *not* interested. Couldn't they see he was only being polite?

I let out a harsh breath. I needed to survive them before I survived the storm tonight.

A woman in her forties approached me. She squirmed in her wetsuit in an attempt to get comfortable I assumed. She glanced at Ethan who was making his way to the next group and gave me a smile.

"Must be hard watching young women fawn all over your husband." She said it loud enough for the young women to hear.

I let out a harsh breath. "You'd think I'd be used to it by now."

"From the look on your face, I'd say not." She patted my arm and walked back to the man she was with.

The two young women spoke animatedly to each other. I spun around and faced the opposite direction, my eyes wide. Why on earth had I just played along? To save Ethan, that's why.

It's not like I was jealous. Ethan was a nice guy and if I could save him from being uncomfortable, I would. I was sure he'd do the same for me. Not that I'd have men fawning over me. And if they showed the faintest interest I'd stay away. Far away. So far, they'd forget I even existed.

I glanced at Ethan. He gave me a lopsided smile, and I couldn't help but return it. I loved the way the upward curve of his lips changed his face, making it softer and happier than he usually seemed. He needed to smile more. Why? I didn't know. The stupid whirlpool of feelings had me thinking crazy things.

We all made our way to the boat and as we headed off, Ethan talked about sea lions.

"Does anyone know the difference between seals and sea lions?"

When he received no answer, he continued, "Two

differences are that sea lions have larger flippers than seals, which means they can walk on land rather than wiggle on their bellies. They also have visible ear flaps." He continued, his animated voice keeping the attention of our guests. Even though I was driving, he always kept my attention too.

ETHAN WAS DOING some work at the table when we got home. His laptop was open in front of him, and he was referring to his iPad as well as shuffling through one of his many piles of paper.

"How did you go with getting everything prepared for the storm?" I asked.

"All sorted. Was the drive home OK?"

"Yes. A bit windy but nothing dramatic."

I passed him as I walked into the kitchen with the kids' lunch boxes and noticed the back of his neck was pink. "Did you forget to put your sunscreen on today?"

He shook his head. "I put it on this morning."

Rose stopped beside him. "Your face is a bit pink and your neck. Did you forget to reapply? I forget to reapply all the time, but Mum reminds me. She also tells me that the UV rays don't hide when it's cloudy."

Ethan touched the back of his neck. "I must have forgotten."

I wonder what he was doing that had him so absent-minded. Probably thinking about the sea lions as he did the things on our storm prep list. "Rose, can you go cut an aloe vera leaf for me and then go and get changed?"

She rushed to the front yard and soon returned with a leaf.

"The aloe vera will help soothe the burn and hopefully

it won't worsen," I said to Ethan. "Take your shirt off and I'll apply it."

Ethan stood and peeled his shirt off. His shoulders were broad up close. Broader than I thought they were, and his waist was slim in comparison. I directed my eyes to the problem area. His neck and shoulders had a pink tinge. Not bad in the scheme of things, probably because he was already tanned.

I squeezed some aloe vera onto his smooth skin. He tensed when it hit and small goose bumps erupted on his flesh. As I rubbed it in, the bumps disappeared. There was a splattering of light freckles on his shoulders that I'd never noticed before. My fingers trailed along the pattern.

"That feels better already," he said.

What was I doing? Not the task I set out to perform. I blushed and finished massaging the aloe in, grateful Ethan had no idea I'd enjoyed touching his skin.

"All done." I stepped away, bumping into the bench. Nothing like drawing attention to myself.

He swung his head in my direction, cocking it. I smiled. At least I hoped it was a smile and not a grimace.

"Thanks." He pulled his t-shirt back on.

I busied myself to give distance between us. Anyone would think I'd never seen a male body up close. He was my co-worker and housemate. I needed to keep my hands to myself. And my thoughts. And everything else.

CHAPTER SIXTEEN

Ethan

Every time thunder struck, Timmy's eyes widened.
They were going to take over his whole face soon. I picked
him up and held him close. Jasmine and Bailey were outside
putting the bikes away. Rose was gathering torches and
placing them on the dining room table.

From where I stood in the dining room, I could see the
rain approaching. It was like a curtain of water pelting
down on the sand. Everything before it was sharp, notice-
able. Everything behind it was hazy.

Where were Jasmine and Bailey? I strode to the front
door. Rose followed.

"Here, take Timmy," I said, handing him to Rose. "Stay
inside. I'll be back in a minute."

I pushed my way out the door. Wind and sand whipped
at my face. A quick scan of the yard showed me that
Jasmine and Bailey weren't there. I spun around and
spotted them at the house next door, clearing away items
the builders had left on their last visit.

I ran over and grabbed Bailey's arm. "Go inside with Rose," I yelled but it still sounded faint. He nodded and ran to the house. I grabbed lengths of wood and dragged them into the house. Jasmine was slamming windows closed. The rain was in the yard now. I ran from window to window, closing them.

Jasmine went outside. "We can't save anything else."

I nodded and grabbed her hand. It was small in mine but strong, like everything else about her. We ran to the house. Rain flew sideways, stinging as it hit my bare skin and following us into the house until I forced the door shut behind us. Puddles formed at our feet.

Jasmine did a quick scan of her children. "Are you OK?"

They nodded. She always thought about them first. Like a good mother should. Like my mother hadn't.

"Timmy has gone into hiding," Rose said.

"I don't blame him." Jasmine smoothed down Rose's hair. She turned to Bailey. "Can you get us some towels, please?"

He was gone before she even finished the sentence. And was back just as quick. He dropped towels on the floor for us to stand on and handed us a towel each. Jasmine's clothes were plastered to her skin, revealing every curve I'd only imagined. Every single one. Heat surged through me. I snapped my mouth shut and turned my attention to drying myself enough to walk to my room to get changed. The only thing better than what I'd just seen would be seeing Jasmine naked.

What the fuck? Mind out of the gutter *now*. This was Jasmine I was thinking about. Jasmine who had children. Jasmine who was only going to be a part of my life for another four months. Jasmine who I worked with.

She was cooking dinner when I came out of my room. The storm was still raging. Rain hammered the windows which rattled from the strength of the wind. Rose and Bailey were playing Snap at the dining room table.

"All the electronics have been unplugged," Jasmine said. "We'll likely lose power from the storm."

A bang on the roof caused Rose to yelp. Bailey tapped the table, demanding her concentration on the game.

Jasmine edged closer to me and whispered, "Rose is not good in storms. When she was four, a bad thing happened during a storm. She doesn't remember it much, but the storm brings her fear back."

I nodded. It must have been bad if the fear stayed with her for five years. "Do you need help?"

"No. I'm nearly done."

I went to the front windows and looked out. It was black out there. Lightning lit up the front yard and beach. Branches were whipped around in the wind. How they didn't snap was beyond me.

"Ethan," Rose said, her voice scared.

I turned back to the table.

"Is there something out there?" Her hands tightened around her cards, bending them.

"No, nothing. Just the storm."

I sat down at the table and watched them play. It was obvious that Bailey was letting his sister win every two or three turns. I glanced back to the window. How could I try to help ease Rose's fear? "My mom loved storms. When I was a kid, we'd go outside to watch them, unless it wasn't safe."

That was one of the good memories I had of my mother. She was usually too self-absorbed to pay us much attention, or obsessed with my father even though he'd treated her like crap.

Rose stared at me with her big blue eyes. "You weren't scared?"

"Sometimes I was."

"What did you do if you were scared?"

"Held my mom's hand tighter." And never tell my dad. Weakness was dangerous.

"If we go to the window, will you hold my hand?"

Jasmine stopped dishing up dinner. Bailey's hand paused in mid-air as he was putting his next card down. I stopped breathing. Rose looked at me with wide, expectant eyes.

"Yes." I wasn't going to deny her, especially when she was being brave like this. To face your fears, even if it's while holding someone's hand, could be life-changing. And she'd chosen to do it with me. I swallowed my anxiety and took a settling breath.

Rose stood up, glancing at Jasmine who gave her a small nod. She held out her hand to me. Bailey put the cards down and watched. My stomach tightened as I stood and took her hand, so tiny. Her eyes rose to mine, and she swallowed. Rumbles of thunder, cracks of lightning and the driving wind didn't drown out my heartbeat. I gave her hand a squeeze.

We walked to the window; with each step, she tightened her grip. I held firm, hoping to convey confidence and safety. Another round of lightning cracked. Rose jumped. She moved closer to me.

"That was a loud one, wasn't it?" I asked.

She nodded.

More lightning. The whole area in front of the house lit up.

"Nothing out there but the storm," I said.

We watched some more as lightning intermittently illuminated the darkness, the pounding water distorting the scene in front of us. I expected her hand to loosen, but it didn't.

"Finished watching?" I asked.

She nodded and led me back to the table. "I still don't like storms."

"You don't have to."

"Dinner's ready," Jasmine said, approaching the table. As she placed my plate in front of me, she whispered in my ear, "Thank you."

My heart swelled. It was as if those two words had imbedded themselves in there and expanded. What was I doing? I was here to research the sea lions not become part of...of what? I glanced around the table. Of *this*.

CHAPTER SEVENTEEN

Jasmine

Bailey and Rose waited for us on the front porch, ready to see what havoc lay in the storm's wake. They chatted non-stop, pointing things out to each other, in animated voices. The road in front of the house had eroded in parts, leaving puddles. Sand was strewn everywhere. Branches and leaves lay in the front yard.

Rose had slept with me all night. The courage Ethan had given her at the window in the middle of the storm hadn't lasted through bedtime. Shock had spread through me when Rose asked Ethan to take her to the window. She'd never wanted to get that close to a storm before. And the fact that he'd said yes and didn't just take her there but stood with her until she was finished, surprised me. He'd started off reserved with the kids. But little by little, he was integrating with them. Men usually tried to brush off children's fears. But Ethan hadn't.

Rose had been calmer after the window but still jumpy.

I knew why. Even if she couldn't remember the incident five years ago, I'd never forget it.

BAILEY WAS TALKING TO SOMEONE. *It wasn't Rose because she was with me in the kitchen. I listened harder. A muffled male voice. "Bailey, who are you talking to?" I asked as I walked into the hallway.*

Bailey had unlocked the front door. It swung open, reverberating as it hit the wall. Max stood on the other side. My throat constricted.

What was he doing here? I had a restraining order against him.

He stepped into the house. I rushed forward and grabbed Bailey, shoving him behind me. I backed up. Step by step. I needed my phone.

Max barged forward. Thunder exploded overhead. I corralled Bailey back, shoving him through the kitchen door. There was not enough space between Max and the children.

"Give me my children," he bellowed.

Thunder overhead. Not even that could drown out his voice. My hands shook. The vibrations spread through my body.

I twisted in the doorway. Bailey stood in the middle of the kitchen, shaking. My mobile phone to his ear. Please tell me he was calling the police.

Where was Rose? I swung around. Where was she?

I needed to stop Max. Or at least slow him down. Give help enough time to arrive. If it was even coming. The kids needed enough time to escape.

I blocked the doorway into the kitchen. Max grabbed me and threw me against the wall. He snatched me on the rebound and smashed me into the door frame.

Lightning cracked, covering the sound of my arm snapping. His grip loosened and I sank to the floor, clutching my arm.

"Bailey. Rose," Max roared, charging past me.

"Run," I screamed as I picked myself up off the floor.

Too late. I was too late. Max yanked Rose off her feet. She screamed. I lunged forward. Bailey turned to his sister. I pushed him toward the front door.

"Run."

Thunder. Lightning. Screaming.

The word Mum on repeat.

I lurched forward. Rose. He needed to let go of Rose. I latched onto Max's arm. A guttural roar escaped his mouth as he shoved me aside. My head smacked into the fridge.

The house was a cacophony of sound. Even the blood rushing in my ears was deafening.

Max was in the hallway, dragging a screaming Rose behind him.

More sound. More light. This time red and blue. Faint. Sirens. Faint.

Help was coming.

But it was too late. Max could get to his car. He could get away.

Bailey ran into the house and grabbed Rose. Max's grip changed as he reached for Bailey. I latched onto Max. He let go of Rose as we tumbled to the ground.

"Run," I screamed.

Bailey grabbed Rose and ran into the rain, into the arms of police officers.

I closed my eyes. I had nothing left; my strength was completely drained.

. . .

ETHAN CAME out into the living room wearing his ranger uniform of boots, long pants and a long-sleeved shirt.

I shook the memory away. "Ready?"

He looked at me closely. "Are you alright?"

I nodded.

He studied me a moment longer before he said, "What's the plan?"

"We need to clear debris off the road, check on the campers and other residents, make sure our infrastructure is OK."

"What about the sea lions?"

It was always the sea lions with him. It didn't bother me like it once would have. It didn't come from a place of self-ishness, but genuine care.

"They're last on the list."

Ethan nodded. I wasn't surprised that he didn't argue. He never did. How hard would it be to hold everything inside all the time? I couldn't do it. I'd done it for ten years with Max and vowed never to lose my voice again.

Ethan joined the kids outside.

"We'll take the ute and load any debris into the back of it," I said.

Bailey spun around, a grin taking over his face. "Are we going to build a bonfire?"

"Sure are."

"Woohoo." He jumped off the porch and started gathering fallen branches.

"Yay," Rose cheered as she followed him. The fear from the storm had passed. Nothing bad had happened. She could rest easy now.

We made our way slowly to the shop, picking up the debris on the way. Most of it was from trees in yards. At each house, I went to see the occupants to make sure they were OK.

The campers in tents had left yesterday when Ethan advised they needed to leave for safety reasons. There was only one caravan left. It was parked next to the bathrooms, using them as a wind shelter.

I approached the owner. "How did you fare in the storm?"

"Quite good. No damage to the van." The lady from the tour stood in the doorway. "I swear I thought the storm was never going to stop."

Bailey ran up to her. "It was gnarly." He swayed like a tree amid the wind.

She laughed, then watched Rose and Ethan carrying a branch to the ute. "Your family had no problems?"

"No, we're experts at storms now."

My family. For the second time, I didn't correct her. I watched Ethan and Rose clearing the grounds. He was always holding himself apart. Not wanting to truly connect, until last night.

"Better go and help," I said. "Call us if you need anything."

"Will do."

We finished the clean-up and headed to the boat. Bailey and Rose put their life jackets on without being asked. Ethan undid the moorings and then stood beside me, scanning the sea, as we made our way to the colony.

We rounded the point. Debris had washed up onto the rocks and sand, but apart from that the area was untouched. I slowed the boat and skimmed the shoreline. A juvenile sea lion lay on his own, away from the others, on the sand. I reached for the binoculars at the same time Ethan did. Our hands brushed. Warmth spread up my arm, and his fingers curled round mine. A wave of energy followed the warmth. I released my grip, almost dropping the binoculars. Stuffing my hands in my pockets, I watched Ethan study the sea lion. His jaw stiffened, hardening every feature on his face. I peered in the direction the binoculars were pointed but couldn't see what caused his reaction.

CHAPTER EIGHTEEN

Ethan

"He's injured. We need to help him." I handed Jasmine the binoculars, making sure not to brush her skin. It had been an accident. But the way she'd jerked away told me the touch had been unwanted.

I stalked to the stairs at the back of the boat.

"You will do no such thing," Jasmine commanded.

I stopped in my tracks. Shit. What was I doing? My jaw flexed.

"They're wild animals, remember?"

I looked back at the sea lion.

She brought the binoculars up to her eyes. For someone so smart, I was acting pretty stupid. How many times had I harped on about them being wild, and interactions with them needing to be limited?

"Firstly, the injury appears to be contained to the blubber. It looks like a clean cut."

I took a deep breath and trudged to her side. She shoved the binoculars into my hands.

"Secondly, look at the sea lion's fin. It has an old injury—a chunk is missing. That's the sea lion you microchipped last week. The one I told you was scared of humans."

Jasmine was right. Anyone would think she had the degree in marine biology, not me. I was an idiot. It was all because I wanted to get away from her touch and the strange feeling it invoked. I wouldn't have acted so rashly otherwise. I never had before.

I shook my head. I hadn't responded to any of her comments. "Yeah, sorry."

What else was there to say? Something more intelligent, perhaps?

I scanned the remaining sea lions. I couldn't see any other injuries.

"Can we go swimming?" Rose asked.

"No, the water is too murky. We can't see what's in there," Jasmine said.

Bailey went to the stairs and studied the water. "Could there be sharks?"

"There could be." Jasmine turned the boat and headed to the other end of the cove. All the sea lions were calm, lounging in the sun.

"We should test the water," I said.

"Why?" Bailey asked, coming to stand beside me.

"The salinity levels of the water can change after a storm. And dirt and sand could be stirred up."

"Is that why the water is murky?"

"Yes."

"Can that hurt the sea lions?"

"It might make it harder for our sea lion friend to heal. It can also clog up the gills of fish, which means they can't breathe and will die."

I pulled out some beakers from my backpack and a refractometer.

"If the fish die, the sea lions won't have anything to eat," Bailey said.

"The sea lions fish in the deeper water."

"We should test that too then," Bailey said.

"Yes, we can do that. We should test it every day to check for changes."

"How do we test it?" he asked, looking at the equipment I'd pulled out of my backpack.

"We'll take a sample of the water in this beaker." I held up the beaker to show him.

Rose came and stood beside him.

"Then we'll collect some of the water and put it in this refractometer." I showed them the piece of equipment that resembled a thin torch. "The refractometer will measure how the light changes when it passes through the water."

Bailey's eyebrows drew together. For a moment, I forgot he was only eleven and not one of my university students. The students I taught at university were older and had a more comprehensive understanding. I needed to explain it in a way he could understand.

"Light travels differently through water with lots of salt than water with a little bit of salt. This instrument can tell us how much salt is in the water by the way the light travels through it. Does that make sense?"

Bailey nodded. I looked at Rose to make sure she understood. She nodded too.

"We can also put samples of the water into these test tubes over the next few days to see how the murkiness changes." I showed them the test tubes. "We'll put the dates on the labels so we know what sample is from what day."

The boat drifted to a stop. Jasmine turned it off and dropped the anchor.

"Why did we stop?" Bailey asked.

"The more we move, the more the water is stirred up. We need to be still when we take the sample, so it's accurate," she said.

Jasmine was a practical thinker. I liked that about her. I liked that she was a great mother and a hard worker. I liked that she would speak out if something bothered her. I liked too much about her. And that was not smart.

I wrote the date on the beaker.

"Can I take the sample?" Bailey asked.

I shook my head. "Not this time. I want to reach down as far as I can. My longer arms are better for that."

"OK."

Most of my students would have been pissy, but he just accepted it. I liked Bailey too; because of his curiosity and willingness to learn. I shook my head. I shouldn't be getting close to them. When the house next door was finished, we could have some degree of separation.

I grabbed my bottle of water and an eyedropper. "I'll show you what the reading is for plain water if you like."

Bailey and Rose nodded eagerly.

"Sit next to me," I said to them.

I opened the angled end of the refractometer, took a sample of water from the bottle with the eyedropper, and then put two drops into the refractometer and closed it. I looked into the device. The numbers read zero.

I handed it over to the children. One by one.

"See how it says zero? That means there's no salt."

They handed it back and I cleaned it. "Now let's do the same for the sea water."

Jasmine watched us with a small smile on her face.

Bailey and Rose concentrated the whole time. Rose wasn't her normal chatterbox self. She listened and took everything in. Their 'wild' label was effectively demolished.

Perhaps it would have been safer for them to remain wild. I'd enjoyed their company all day. And most other days. It was dangerous to get close, but for some unfathomable reason, I just couldn't help it.

CHAPTER NINETEEN

Jasmine

As Ethan, Bailey and Rose collected water and tested it, Ethan answered their questions patiently and thoughtfully. If something he said wasn't age-appropriate, he'd rephrase it. Warmth spread through me as I watched them interact with each other.

Ethan was great with children. He was kind and patient. Why hadn't he and his wife had any?

Ethan ruffled Bailey's hair. "Thanks for helping."

He turned to Rose and gave her a fist bump. "You did a good job."

Rose grinned at me, and my heart swelled. She had always been confident with Bailey and me, confident as a team. Being recognised on her own for her own effort was rare. Ethan had done that for her.

I turned the boat for home. We'd tested the water in the bay and out deeper. I glanced back at Ethan. He was sitting with the children. None of them said a word, content with the silence. Had my determination not to fall into another relationship denied my children this?

Ethan and Max were such contrasts. Ethan was reserved, whereas Max forced himself into every situation, especially if he thought it benefited him. Ethan took his time teaching the children, whereas Max would have expected them to just do as they were told. Max would never have acknowledged their questions as Ethan had done, being patient and nurturing to their curiosity.

The children had never mattered to Max. He'd been the most important person in the world to himself. He always wanted to be the centre of attention and would change friends frequently to make sure he was. We were not important unless we elevated his position.

I could have lived with all of that if it was just me. But it wasn't just me. And I hated the way he treated the children.

"Is there anything else we need to do today?" Ethan asked from beside me.

I jumped. I hadn't heard him coming. "Just need to cancel the tours until Monday, but that's it."

"Is it OK if I leave that with you? I'd like to record all our findings from today."

What a change. I doubt he would have asked back when he started.

"Of course. Why don't you head back home to do that? I'll take the kids with me to give you some peace."

"Great. Thanks," he said with a smile. When he smiled, his entire face brightened—his cheeks lifted and filled, his eyes crinkled. It was the type of smile you automatically returned.

He stayed beside me as we headed to the jetty, his warmth seeping into me, spreading through my body. It was delicious. I snuck a glance up at him. He was watching me with those vibrant hazel eyes. My stomach swirled, and I tore my gaze away.

I wasn't attracted to Ethan. So why was my body saying otherwise?

CHAPTER TWENTY

Ethan

I WALKED BACK to the house alone, relishing the peace. But it wasn't the peace of being alone. It was the peace of the whole day. Could that be classified as the best day I'd had since I got here?

After I'd made the mistake with the sea lion, Jasmine hadn't got hung up on it. Audrey would have. She would have made small jibes for the rest of the afternoon. She'd always been jealous of my success.

The jibes were often about my failures. And one of those failures was not climbing out from my father's influence. She liked to point out whenever I acted like him. I'd learnt at a young age to shut down my feelings and my reactions. I'd mastered that in adulthood. The only time I felt free was with the sea lions, whether it be interacting with them or studying them.

Today I felt free for a different reason—peace and contentment. And it came from the three people I least expected. I didn't know whether to grab onto it and relish it or run the other way. I couldn't run far. Not when I lived with them. Maybe I could just enjoy what we had. If I did, I needed to be conscious of my behaviour at all times. I didn't want anyone to get hurt.

Timmy met me as I made my way to my room to grab my laptop. He stretched each of his legs as he walked. I chuckled. He had grown in the two months I'd been here, but lost none of his character. He followed me all the way to my room and back to the kitchen table. I pulled out a chair for him and he sat beside me as I worked, getting lost in the figures and data.

I heard Bailey and Rose before I saw them. Rose was chatting away. Timmy heard them as well and ran to the door to meet them. When they entered, he weaved between their legs.

"Mum had to help a new camper," Bailey said. "She sent us home to help you with dinner."

I closed my laptop. "Go, wash your hands and we'll get started on the Mission Burritos." I got the ingredients out. "Let's start with the marinade," I said as they joined me at the counter.

I read out the ingredients to them and they added them to the bowl.

There was a knock at the front door. My hands were covered in marinade.

"Bailey, can you get that, please?"

I washed my hands as he answered the door.

"Hi, Bailey," a man's voice said.

Bailey slammed the door, turned around and froze. All the blood had drained from his face. I rushed to him and bent to look at him.

"Bailey, what's wrong?"

"It's my dad."

The knock sounded again. Bailey nearly jumped out of his skin. He stared at me the same way Steve did when our father was on a rampage. I steeled myself.

"One minute," I called out.

I turned to Rose. She was staring at us.

"I'm going outside to speak to him."

Bailey's eyes widened and he sucked in a shaky breath. I placed my hands on his shoulders.

"I want you to call your mum. Tell her to come in the back way." I stood up.

"Don't go out there," Bailey said, his voice trembling.

"I'll be OK."

"He'll trick you. You'll let him in."

I crouched down to his level. "I won't let him trick me. I know what bad men are like."

My dad was one.

"Call your mum. Lock the doors. Close the windows. No matter what happens, don't come out."

He nodded. I stood up and opened the door, stepped through and closed it behind me.

CHAPTER TWENTY-ONE

Jasmine

My hands shook as I opened the back door. I searched the room for Rose and Bailey. They were at the kitchen counter and came running when they saw me. I caressed their heads.

"Are you OK?"

Rose nodded.

Bailey looked toward the front. "Ethan is out there." He clutched at my arm. "I think Dad has tricked him, I heard Ethan laugh."

Fuck. That man could wield charming as if it were a spell. Not even Ethan, who knew him for less than ten minutes, seemed immune to it.

"I'm going outside."

Rose started to shake.

"It's OK. Ethan is out there. He's big and strong. He's not scared of anything."

Max may have convinced him I was crazy and the bad guy. But I wasn't going to tell the kids that. What was I going to do if Ethan believed Max and sided with him? I would do what I was put on Earth to do. I would protect my children.

"If you hear fighting, I want you to go out the back door and run to Jack and Lily's. You understand?"

Bailey nodded.

There was no point calling the police. They were too far away. And I didn't know how this situation was going to turn out. I didn't want to call them for no reason.

I caressed their heads again. "It will be OK."

I took deep breaths as I made my way to the door, clenching and unclenching my hands. I knew this day would come. I'd prepared for it in my head. I'd prepared the words I was going to say over and over again.

Max had been released from prison two months ago. I was surprised it took him this long to turn up. I'd been so distracted by Ethan and work that I'd barely thought about it. And the longer it took for him to arrive, the more wishful thinking I had that he wouldn't.

I opened the door and stepped out. Ethan and Max were sitting on the porch chairs, slightly turned into each other but not directly facing one another. Max looked the same as he always did—blonde, windswept hair, piercing blue eyes. Jail hadn't changed him a bit. The outside was still the same but what about the inside? Could a man like Max ever change?

Ethan watched me and then stood and came to my side, taking my hand in his. His hand didn't swallow mine, it joined it. My shoulders relaxed. The simple act told me everything I needed to know. He was here for me.

Max's shrewd eyes went to our hands and the way his eyebrows turned down told me he had been expecting to find me alone. He stood. His height, his broadness, may have been intimidating if I'd been alone. But Ethan matched him for both. The only difference was Max wielded his size for power, and Ethan never thought of his as anything special.

"Hi, Jasmine."

Words stuck in my throat. I stared at him.

Ethan gave my hand a squeeze. "Max was just telling me about the time Bailey tried to cut his hair so he could look like Max."

I nodded. Interesting how he thought of *that* story to share. Like it showed he had some special connection with Bailey. I bet he didn't tell Ethan how he had berated Bailey afterwards. Or how he made snide remarks to a five-year-old about how he would never be as good as him.

Max took a step forward. "How have you been? How are Bailey and Rose?"

"We're good, thanks." He didn't deserve any more than that.

"Ethan tells me you're the head ranger here."

"That's correct."

"You always loved nature. We did some great bush walks in Adelaide."

I wouldn't have called the two we went on great. He'd made the whole thing miserable.

"I bet the kids love it too," he added.

"They do."

Max took another step forward. My heart slammed against my chest wall. My palm sweated against Ethan's. His grip firmed, giving me the strength to straighten my back.

Max made eye contact with me. "I'd like to see them."

"That won't be happening today." I was shaking on the inside, but my voice was firm.

"I drove nearly eight hours to see them." There was a tic in his jaw, but his voice remained passive. He hadn't lost his skill.

"If you'd called, I would have told you not to come."

"I'm here now though. It's been five years. I've missed them."

That wasn't true. He'd asked about us initially trying to get information from his family. But that hadn't lasted. If he'd missed them, he would have been craving information, begging for it. He hadn't asked about us in nearly four years.

Ethan turned his body slightly toward me, bringing himself closer. A protective move? I wanted to lean into him, to soak up what he was offering me.

I gave Max my full attention. "You will not be seeing Bailey and Rose today. I will have my solicitor contact you."

There went the tic in his jaw again. "Come on, Jazzy." I cringed at the use of that name. "We don't need a solicitor."

Maybe he didn't, but I did.

Ethan took a deep breath and glanced at me. I looked up at him, my jaw set. He squared his shoulders. "This is something we've discussed as a family," he said. "*Jasmine* and I won't be changing our minds."

Max looked between us. Tic. Tic. Tic.

"I'll have the solicitor contact you," I said.

"Can I just say hello to them?"

Ethan released my hand and pointed to the stairs. I immediately missed his touch, and his gentle strength, but the hard edge to his voice when he next spoke gave all that back to me. "Not today." When Max didn't budge, he said, "Best you leave now."

Tic. Tic. Tic. Max nodded and walked down the stairs.

"It was nice to meet you, Max," Ethan said to his retreating back.

He got nothing in return.

Ethan turned to me. "Go talk to Bailey and Rose. I'll wait out here."

I forced my feet to move as I tried to reconcile what had just happened. Lingering, trying to figure it out, was less important than making sure the kids were OK. Thinking about how Ethan and I had stood together as one against Max would need to wait.

CHAPTER TWENTY-TWO

Ethan

WHAT WAS I THINKING, getting myself into the middle of a situation I should only want to avoid? I'd pretended they were my family. My family. But a person like me shouldn't have a family.

Max was exactly like my father. I knew it the moment he opened his mouth. I probably wouldn't have known it straight away if it hadn't been for Bailey's terror and his warning not to be tricked. But I would have recognised it soon enough.

He'd played a good game. He hadn't played the victim straight up. First, he'd scoped me out, then dropped little hints to see if I would be sympathetic. He hadn't mentioned Bailey and Rose as individuals, but rather how they pertained to him.

He had the classic traits of a narcissist. I should know. My father was one. And if I didn't keep such control over myself, I'd likely be one too. This family did not need to swap one out for another. The difference between me, and

Max and my father, was that I knew what I was. And because of that, I would need to keep my distance while I kept all of them safe. I could protect Jasmine, Bailey and Rose without losing myself to them.

But what would Jasmine think? I'd just inserted myself into this whole situation without discussing it with her first. Would she think I was trying to take away her power?

The front door opened, and Jasmine stepped out. "They're OK. Scared but OK."

Good. That's all we could hope for under the circumstances. Not *we*. Jasmine. It's all *Jasmine* could hope for.

We sat on the chairs, and she gave me a small smile. "Thank you for your support."

I breathed a sigh of relief. "Sorry about inserting myself into the situation."

Jasmine studied me. "I'm glad you did. It helped me be strong."

"You don't need my help with that. You're a strong, independent person."

She looked down at her feet. "Not always with Max. Five years ago, I decided to leave him. I saw what he was doing to the children, how he'd destroyed their confidence." She twisted her toes into the deck before returning her gaze to me. "He sensed something was going on. I don't know if someone let it slip while I was making plans. I'd been putting money away little by little for months. Then I started looking for a place to live. He started making promises that he was going to change. His *changes* would last for a week or so."

She sighed, then shrugged. I knew how her story would end. I'd seen it more than once with my parents. The broken promises. The blame. More broken promises. It was never-ending.

"Then it was my fault when he failed and next he started blaming the kids. We all walked on eggshells. It strengthened my resolve." She took a shaky breath. "I didn't fight back, didn't try to argue. I knew it would make it worse. But it got worse anyway. He told anyone who would listen that I was a bad wife and an even worse mother."

She met my eyes and took a deep breath. Her hands were shaking. I reached out and took them. She latched on. "I left. He got worse. He'd turn up when I was shopping, watch me at the hairdresser, catch my train in the morning, follow me home from work. I was so scared. I didn't know what he was capable of anymore, so I got a restraining order. He got worse." Her voice swayed between fear and restrained anger. "He told me he was going to take the kids from me. I got a solicitor involved. He didn't like that. His next play was to take Bailey and Rose."

She took a wavering breath. "He nearly did. He turned up one night during a storm."

As she told me what happened, my grip tightened. Rose's fear of storms became clear. Bailey's warning not to be tricked made sense. Jasmine's bravery was her biggest strength.

I didn't let go of her hands. "I wish my mom had been as brave as you." I took a deep breath and let it out slowly. Should I tell her more? Not for me but for her. To show her what her strength achieved. "We endured my father for sixteen years. The day she died, we all got freedom. She left this world and my brother and I left our father."

Saying it out loud was hard. I forced myself to keep eye contact with her. I wasn't embarrassed, but it was a part of my life I'd rather forget. The problem was the fear of being like my father never left me. It was the lasting legacy of a man I'd rather not remember.

CHAPTER TWENTY-THREE

Jasmine

MY BREATH FALTERED. Sixteen years. Ethan had been forced to survive someone like Max for sixteen years? And as a child? I hugged him tight. One hug couldn't erase his pain, but I wanted it to. Until I realised how inappropriate hugging him was. Just because he had posed as my partner didn't mean I had the right to touch him like that or any other way. I pulled away.

"What are you going to do now?" he asked.

I shrugged. "My first reaction is to run."

I searched his face. The mask was back; I couldn't read him. His one moment of vulnerability was gone.

"Do you want to do that?" he asked.

I sighed. "No. We have a good life here."

He nodded. "Do you think Max has changed?"

"I'd like to think he has, for the children's sake. But I don't know."

"People like Max rarely change."

How many times had his dad promised to change and

then disappointed them? Max had promised so many times. In the end, he believed it more than I did.

"Above all, I need to protect Bailey and Rose. I'll call my solicitor on Monday to get advice. I'm not going to deal with him directly. It's too risky for me and the children if he hasn't changed. If he's serious, he'll do what he has to, starting with following my solicitor's instructions." I stood up. I took a shallow breath and made eye contact with him before saying, "We'll need to pretend to be in a relationship all the time. You never know when he'll be watching."

Ethan grinned. And damn, it was charming.

"Shouldn't be hard. You put me in my place enough. And you've already told people I'm your husband."

I blushed. I didn't think he'd heard me. "I, ah, I was just trying to get those women to back off."

Ethan cocked his head. "Jealous, were you?"

"No." My reply was so quick I even doubted it. I opened the door, but Ethan didn't move to follow me. "Are you coming?"

"I'm going to check the windows and doors first."

"Thank you."

He walked down the stairs, and while the view was nice, I had to admit, he was more than sex on legs. There were so many layers behind the one he presented to the world. A pain he hid down deep. Pain that now may be exposed because he chose to stand with me against Max. The risk he was taking for me, for us, was huge.

"If you change your mind, it's OK."

"I won't." He was firm in his answer. I believed him.

Tonight was going to be restless for more than one reason. What would dominate my thoughts? Max's sudden reappearance or Ethan being my fake boyfriend?

THE NEXT MORNING, Ethan walked into the kitchen and glanced at the children, who sat quietly at the table, before coming to stand beside me.

"Coffee?" I asked.

"Yes, please."

I yawned.

"Didn't sleep well?"

I shook my head. "I don't think they did either."

"Makes four of us then."

Rose's trauma bear sat in her lap. A police officer had given it to her the day Max tried to abduct them. For a year, she'd slept with the bear every night and carted it with her everywhere. From then until last night, it had sat on her bedhead watching over her.

I added some extra coffee to the cup. "I'd like to take the kids to school today so I can explain what's happening to the principal."

Ethan took the cup from my hand. My fingers lingered. I needed to feel his steadiness. Yesterday, I'd scrambled away from his touch. Today I was seeking it out. I withdrew my hand. My tired brain was confusing fear for connection.

"And I'd like to make contact with the police. The restraining order has run out, but I'd like them to be aware of what's happening in case I need to reapply."

"I'll cover the morning tour," Ethan said.

"Thank you. That will give me time to speak to their bus driver as well." I put bread in the toaster for Bailey and Rose. "It will be your first tour on your own."

Ethan gave me a lopsided smile. "How will I ever cope without my wife?"

"I'm sure you are fully capable."

Ethan was capable of many things, making me feel safe and supported were two of them.

"So are you. You're a great mom, Jasmine. Trust your instincts."

There he went again with the compliments.

My instincts were telling me to trust Ethan. But the whirlpool of feelings had returned, sucking me into it, confusing me. Were my feelings real, or a product of my fears? Would my instincts keep me safe or lead to further pain?

CHAPTER TWENTY-FOUR

Ethan

A LIGHT FOG surrounded the bay. San Francisco often had fog, but it was nothing like this. Here the fog was delicate, like the white sand on the beach that often blew into house yards. The thick rolling fog that surrounded my home city was chilly and had a briny smell. Sometimes it was so dense the foghorn would be used on repeat. I smiled. That foghorn was the sound of home. I hardly ever noticed it anymore, like most locals. The same way someone who lived near train tracks wouldn't notice trains going past.

The tourists were waiting at the meeting point.

"Good morning, everyone," I said, glancing around at the smiling faces in the small group. "We have some light fog over the bay today, but this won't affect our tour. I imagine it will dissipate soon. Does anyone know how fog is created?"

Heads shook.

"Well, this one had the perfect conditions of a clear sky and light wind. Warm, moist air travelled over the cooler water. The water cooled the air. When the air cools, the invisible water vapour turns into tiny water droplets we can see."

The small group stared out over the bay. I continued with our usual tour. Running a tour on my own was harder than I imagined. Jasmine had this amazing ability of keeping the tour flowing and everyone organised. I felt like it was mayhem. I tried to have engaging conversations while keeping an eye on the swimmers and sea lions.

I missed her small nods of reassurance and her laughter at the sea lions' antics. It must have been my tired brain. I'd never missed her before. When we arrived back at the dock, Jasmine was waiting for us. She gave everyone a smile as they disembarked and headed to the change room.

"How did it go?" she asked, taking one of the bags of snorkelling gear from me.

"It's much easier with two people."

She nodded. "That's why I reduced the size of the afternoon tours. It was too hard on my own."

Guilt stabbed me. It was because I took the afternoons for my research that she had to work on her own. She'd even blocked tours on Tuesday and Wednesday, the quietest days, so I could have the boat if I needed it. I'd grumbled to myself about her lack of support when she'd been giving it to me all along.

We unpacked the boat and started washing all the gear while the guests returned their wetsuits one by one. Then we hosed those off and hung them to dry in the shed.

When we finished, Jasmine said, "Let's head to the store. I want to let Jack and Lily know about Max."

"OK. How did it go at the school?"

"The principal said she would call a meeting with the staff to discuss the situation. The teachers will keep a close eye on Bailey and Rose and will let us know of any changes in their behaviour."

"That's good."

"And the bus driver said he will make sure I'm there to pick the kids up before he drops them off."

Jasmine was so proactive, unlike my mother. She'd never put any actions in place. And had never protected me or my brother from our father's behaviour. I'd done the protecting by sheltering Steve as much as I could and always making sure he was OK.

We walked up the stairs together and through the door. Jack was stacking the fridge and turned to greet us.

"Is Lily about?" Jasmine asked.

"Lily," Jack called out. "Jasmine and Ethan are here."

Thirty seconds later she appeared. She glanced between us, her eyes narrowing. "What's up?"

"My ex, Max, turned up yesterday wanting to see the kids."

Jack stood up taller, his face tense. I'd never seen him serious before, not even when he was doing a crossword. "Did you let him?"

"No. I told him I would contact my solicitor."

Jack nodded. "And he accepted that?"

"Not really. He tried to cajole me."

Lily clasped her hands together so tight her forearms flexed.

"Ethan pretended we were a couple," Jasmine said, "and told him we'd discussed it as a family."

Lily smiled at me. I couldn't decipher its meaning.

"And then what?" Jack asked.

"Ethan told him to leave, and he did."

I took a deep breath. "He'll be back. Men like Max don't give up easily."

"So now we need to pretend that we're a couple," Jasmine said, looking at me.

I wasn't sure if she meant it to sound like a question or an invitation. Did she doubt what I'd said last night? Did she think I'd have second thoughts?

I moved closer to her, hoping she'd feel my determination. "It won't be hard. We live and work together." I took her hand. "And she already refers to me as her husband."

Lily's eyebrows shot up. Jack considered us.

Jasmine laughed. "I agreed to that to protect you from women who can't stop staring at you."

My stomach lifted. I gave her a nudge. "But you didn't deny it."

"Perhaps she wanted to keep you for herself," Lily said, waggling her eyebrows.

I could only wish. I gave my head a small shake. What on Earth was I thinking?

Jasmine let go of my hand. "Anyway, please keep an eye out for Max and let us know if you see him."

She gave them descriptions of him and the car he'd been driving.

"We can help with the kids too. Keep an eye on them when you're working," Lily said.

Jasmine shook her head. "That's OK. They can just stay at the office when I'm at work."

Lily stepped forward. "Jasmine, we will help." Her voice was firm. "The kids do not need to be cooped up in an office after being at school all day."

Jack took his place by her side. "Absolutely. One of us can sit on the porch while they play on the beach."

Jasmine opened her mouth in what I was sure would be a protest. I didn't let her get that far. "That would be great," I said. "And they can help me with my research."

Jasmine swung around, her mouth agape.

I shrugged. "They were helpful over the weekend. If they get too restless, they can go for a swim."

Lily clapped her hands together. "That's settled then. You can't do this on your own. We're family and we're going to help."

Tears brimmed Jasmine's eyes. "Thank you."

Jack grinned. "Bonfire night on Saturday. Let's show everyone you're a couple."

Jasmine and I locked eyes. What was Jack up to?

CHAPTER TWENTY-FIVE

Jasmine

Bailey, who was usually jumping out of his skin for bonfire night, sat on the lounge watching TV.

"Bails, are you ready?" I asked.

He shrugged. I sat down beside him. Ethan hung back in the kitchen, watching.

"What's wrong?" I asked.

"Nothing."

Rose brought Timmy into the lounge room. She sat down on a lounge chair, watching us. Her trauma bear was in her lap again. Timmy sat obediently beside her. Still, Bailey said nothing. He continued to stare at the TV.

How was I going to get this eleven-year-old to use his words? "When we're nervous about something it's always better to speak about it."

Bailey looked at Ethan. Was he nervous about him? Ethan gave him a nod.

Bailey glanced between us as he spoke. "What if Dad turns up at the bonfire? Or if he comes to the house?"

I rested my hand on his leg. "If he comes to the bonfire, he can't hurt us. There will be too many people there."

"There aren't people here," Bailey said.

Rose pulled Timmy toward her and held him tight.

"No. But we're safe together."

"We weren't safe last time."

Ethan came and sat on the other lounge chair. "Your mom would do anything to keep you safe."

My heart swelled.

Ethan had Bailey's undivided attention. "She will always protect you. She's kept you safe all these years."

Bailey nodded. "And you will help keep us safe too?"

"Yes, I will."

Ethan said it with such certainty that none of us could doubt him.

"Will you keep Mum safe?" Bailey asked. "Dad hurt her bad last time."

"I will do everything in my power to keep your mom safe."

I glanced at Rose. She was holding Timmy and the bear to her chest. How much did she remember now that she'd seen Max again? She'd blocked it out afterwards. The psychologist said that was normal.

Ethan stood up. "We're a team, right?"

Bailey nodded. Ethan turned his attention to Rose. She smiled.

"OK team, let's check the windows and doors and get out of here."

As we were leaving the house, Ethan held me back. "You go on ahead. I want to check the house next door and lock it up."

I broke into a sweat. I flicked my eyes to the house and back at him. "I don't want you to go in there alone."

He took hold of my arm. Gentle but firm, as if he was requesting understanding not demanding it. "I need to make sure, Jasmine. I don't want you and the kids here when I do it."

"Come with us and bring Jack back with you," I pleaded.

Ethan turned me to face him. "No." He glanced at the children. "I don't want them to think this house is something else to be scared of."

The house I once wished he'd move into and now, I wished he never would. "OK."

"I won't be long. I'll catch up soon."

"OK."

My feet were rooted to the ground. All I wanted to do was hug him and feel the safety of his arms. He released my arm and turned me to the children. I took a step towards them and then another.

"I'm going to lock up the other house and I'll meet you there," he said as casually as can be.

"We'll get the best spot." I slung his chair over my shoulder and then addressed the children. "Not too close to the fire."

They walked on ahead of me, and I glanced back at Ethan who was watching us leave. I took a deep breath. He would be fine. It was just my nerves. When I looked again, he was walking up the stairs.

By the time we got to the bonfire site on the beach in front of the store, Ethan had not caught up. I studied the empty roadway. Where was he? My heart pounded an erratic beat like waves during a storm. I set up our chairs, my gaze continually flicking toward the road.

"Waiting for your husband?" Jack asked from beside

me. I jumped. I'd been concentrating too hard on Ethan's return to notice Jack's approach.

"He's locking up the other ranger house."

"Good idea."

"He's taking longer than I thought."

Jack squeezed my shoulder. "The windows probably got stuck. They would have expanded after the storm."

"Yeah. Probably." Except we hadn't reopened them.

They hadn't been stuck the last time we'd closed them. Rose was sitting next to Lily, telling her some kind of story. Bailey was helping Ross fill the Esky.

"I'm going to see if he needs any help," I said.

"Ethan is a big boy. I'm sure he can lock up on his own. Go and have a chin wag with Lily."

But I couldn't stop watching for him.

Jack blew out a breath. "You can watch the road from the chair next to Lily."

I nodded. I was being silly. There were a million reasons why Ethan hadn't arrived yet. A million reasons other than Max. I took a seat half listening to the conversation.

"Is Sara making us fish and chips?" Rose asked.

"She's heating up the fryers as we speak," Lily said.

Rose clapped.

There was movement from the road.

CHAPTER TWENTY-SIX

Ethan

As I approached the bonfire, Jack came over to greet me. I still had the shakes.

"Fuck me. The spider was bigger than my hand," I said to Jack with a shiver.

Jack guffawed. "Small then."

"Small my ass. And it just stood there in the doorway, blocking my path."

"What'd you do? Stare it down?" Jack was still laughing.

"What else was I going to do?"

Everyone was watching the interaction now, even the campers and house guests.

"Ah, move it."

"I wasn't going near the thing. It was so big I could see the hair on its legs."

Jack turned to Jasmine. "Seems like he needed you to save him, after all."

Bailey stood beside Jasmine and put his arm across her

shoulders. "Mum's not scared of spiders. She picks them up and takes them outside."

Rose stood on the other side of Jasmine and put her arm on top of Bailey's. "Mum's not scared of anything."

Jasmine caught my eye and then looked at each of the children. "It's OK to be scared."

"Even adults?" Rose asked.

"Even adults."

Rose came over to me and put her small hand in mine. "We're a team, Ethan. Mum will protect you from the spiders. And you will protect us."

I crouched down. "The spiders are pretty scary."

She patted my shoulder. "So are storms."

I held out my hand to her. "Team?"

She gave it a hard shake. "Team."

Until the crisis passed. Then I could go back to my life where I didn't need to be scared of being like my father. And after that, I would return home.

Jack led me over to Ross and Jay who were handing out drinks. I took a beer, and we stood together in a small huddle.

"Jack has told us what's going on," Ross said. "If you need anything come to the house."

"Thank you." I knew they meant it. They loved Jasmine and the kids like they were family.

"How are the kids holding up?" Jack asked.

"They're a bit rattled."

Jack nodded. "That's to be expected."

"We're trying to make everything as normal as we can. But how can we when they are used to living so free and now, we lock the windows and doors?"

Jack gave an understanding nod. "To make it worse, it will be school holidays soon."

I hadn't thought of that. Shit. They couldn't be house-bound for weeks on end. We would all go crazy.

Footsteps approached. I turned to see Sara crossing the road with a trolley filled with wrapped paper parcels.

"Who's ready for the best fish and chips in Haven Bay?" she called out.

"Me." Rose jumped up and ran to Sara.

Sara squeezed her shoulder. "You'll get yours quicker if you help me hand them out. Then I can go back and cook some more."

Rose grabbed a parcel, looked at the name, and delivered it to the owner. When Jasmine received hers, she moved to our seats and I followed.

"A spider, huh?" she asked, a small smile on her face.

"It was no ordinary spider."

She nodded. "It is Australia."

I laughed. "Maybe it was an ordinary Australian spider."

Rose approached with a parcel for her, Bailey and me. But Bailey wasn't in sight. I scanned the crowd, my gaze darting from person to person until I found him talking to Ross. I let out a breath. I needed to calm down. We were here with friends. Everyone was safe. And Max was nowhere to be seen.

I glanced at Rose. She was studying me, her eyes drifting to Bailey and back to me. Rose pulled her chair closer to mine. "Do you think my father is here?"

I placed a chip in my mouth and chewed slowly. Funny how I referred to them as chips now, not fries. I surveyed our surroundings. Her words *my father* and the fact that there was no warmth in her voice reflected their relationship. She was nine years old, energetic and bubbly, but she had a wisdom about her.

I moved my attention to her. I wasn't going to betray her trust by lying to her. "I thought he might be, but I've looked for him but haven't seen him."

"He could be hiding."

"He could be. But I don't think so."

"How can you be sure?"

I indicated around the big circle of people. "Someone would have seen him."

She nodded, then picked up a chip, popped it in her mouth and said, "Mmm. It's hella good."

Jasmine leant over. Her body heat seeped through me, more powerful than the fire in front of us. I could have been sitting in the middle of the fire and the heat from Jasmine still would have been stronger.

"Thank you," she whispered in my ear. Her soft breath was a caress against my skin. I faced her. Our lips were an inch apart, the air between them warm and rousing. I licked my lips. My eyes dropped to hers and then up to her brown eyes which were wide, perhaps in question. My breath caught.

What? Was I supposed to be saying something? Right, she'd just thanked me.

"You're welcome," I squeezed out.

What was going on with my brain? We were pretending to be a family. Pretending. Right?

CHAPTER TWENTY-SEVEN

Jasmine

Jack cracked a grin as I walked into the shop. "You and Ethan seemed pretty close last night."

What was he even talking about?

I narrowed my eyes. "That's what happens when you sit next to each other."

Lily appeared and stood beside him. Her curls were extra bouncy today as she looked between us.

"Jack wasn't talking about you sitting next to each other." The lilt in her voice matched her curls.

"Hell no. You two were in your own little world."

"Speaking to each other," I said.

"Getting lost in each other's eyes." Jack pretended to stare dreamily into Lily's.

I shook my head. "Have you been swapping your thriller books for Lily's romances?"

"Don't need a romance book to see what's going on between the two of you."

"We sat next to each other and had a conversation. Nothing unusual there."

"She doth protest too much," Jack said, and Lily nodded.

"Whatever. I'm here to collect the mail."

"It's Sunday, love," Jack said.

Shit. My brain was not functioning.

"She's distracted by love." Jack held a hand to his heart.

Lily giggled, actually giggled.

"Lucky that house next door isn't finished, huh?" Jack said. The suggestiveness in his voice insinuated I thought it was more than convenient.

I rolled my eyes and walked out. Their laughter followed me down the stairs. I was distracted, but it had nothing to do with Ethan or the way he'd looked at me last night. I told myself that all the way to the office. We were finishing a couple of things off before the Sunday tour. The kids were with Jay and Ross.

Ethan and I worked in silence. He stared at his screen, shook his head and then typed, his fingers tapping keys quickly. I studied him as he hit backspace over and over.

"What's got you so worked up?" I asked.

"A review."

"A review about what?"

"Our tour."

I stood up and made my way over to him. "What about our tour?"

He let out a harsh breath. "We are disorganised, we share dull facts, we—"

"Bullshit," I said as I reached his side and read the review over his shoulder. It was worse than that. According to the reviewer, we had no personality and paid more attention to each other than we did the guests.

"That's crap. Who is the review from?"

"I can't tell. Mr R is all it says."

"Does it say what date he toured?"

Ethan shook his head. He clicked on the reviewer's name. There were no other reviews. And he had no posts about other places he visited.

"Are you responding?"

"I thought about it, but I wouldn't want to antagonise Mr R." Ethan took hold of my arm and gave it a gentle squeeze. "Don't worry about it. Every other review is glowing."

I nodded. It was disappointing but what could we do? Apologise online for something that wasn't true?

"Jasmine." His voice was commanding yet soft.

I made eye contact with him, and my stomach lifted as if a buoy in the ocean. Gosh, his hazel eyes were beautiful. More green than brown. Jack's conversation reeled around my brain. I broke eye contact. I was not lost in Ethan's eyes.

He squeezed my arm again. "A low review gives legitimacy to all the others."

"How do you figure?"

"No one's perfect."

"Yeah, but—"

Heavy footsteps sounded on the stairs before the screen door opened, and Max stepped inside. The buoy was punctured, and my stomach plummeted. His eyes narrowed as he glanced between us. I stood up straight.

"Hi, Jasmine. Ethan." His voice hardened on Ethan's name.

"Max," I said, not moving.

What was he doing here? How did he know we were in the office? I glanced out the window, trying not to make it obvious. The kids weren't on the beach. Hopefully, Jay was entertaining them inside.

Ethan stayed seated.

"I've brought gifts for Bailey and Rose. Can I see them?"

I glanced at his hands. A teddy and fishing rod.

I clenched my hands. "I told you that my solicitor would contact you. She sent a letter last week."

His jaw stiffened. "It's been five years. Surely they're ready by now."

"Surely, you want to do it the right way." My voice was tinged with sarcasm. "After all, it's been five years."

There went the tic in his jaw.

Ethan touched my leg. It was subtle, but I got the hint loud.

I took a deep breath. What would Ethan say? Then I did my best Ethan impression. "I'm sorry you drove all this way, Max. I think it's important for the children that we go through the correct processes."

"Important for the children or for you?"

"Both, actually. It's my job to keep them safe."

He took a step forward. Ethan shifted in his seat but didn't get up.

"I'm their father." Max glanced at Ethan. Although his face was placid, his message was clear.

I didn't care. I knew which one I'd rather be their father.

"Max, the last time the children saw you, you were taken away by the police. How do you think that made them feel?"

"How do you think it made me feel?"

It always turned back around to him. He was insinuating it was my fault. He didn't need to say the words.

"Bailey and Rose were traumatised by that night. It will take time to rebuild a relationship."

"That's why I'm here."

I took a deep breath. How I ever married him was beyond me. I must have been pretty bloody stupid.

Ethan's feet moved. Heels raised and placed back down again. The muscles in his legs tensed. But his upper body stayed relaxed. "Jasmine has given you her answer." His voice was calm, light.

"Can I at least give them the gifts?"

"You can leave the gifts here. I will give them to them when I think it's appropriate," I said.

"In other words, never."

"When it's *appropriate*."

Max's fingers tightened around the teddy's arm, crushing it. They wouldn't want his gifts. Rose had her trauma bear who could never be replaced. And Bailey didn't like fishing.

Ethan stood. "Is there anything else you'd like today, Max?"

Max retrained his face. His jaw relaxed. His eyes calmed. "Other than seeing my children, no."

Ethan moved closer to me so that our arms were touching, tethering us to each other.

"I'm sorry we can't make that happen today. I think the best thing to do would be to answer the solicitor's letter."

Max glanced between us. Whether he saw a formidable team or something else was unclear.

"OK. I'll leave these here with you for when you think it's *appropriate*." He placed them on my desk and walked out.

Ethan went to the door and watched him. My legs were shaking as I sat down in Ethan's chair with a sigh. He'd let me handle Max. Just that alone made me feel capable and strong. Ethan stayed by the door but faced me. I took a breath in and closed my eyes. The strength I'd shown moments ago seeped from my body.

"You did good," Ethan said.

I opened my eyes and gave him a weary smile. "I don't know what I would have done if you weren't here."

"I didn't do anything. You were standing your ground."

I blew out a breath. "He wasn't going to give up."

Ethan smiled. "Neither were you. I only said something because it was obvious it was going nowhere."

I nodded. "Thank you."

He shrugged. "I didn't want him to ruin the good vibes in our office."

I laughed. "The good vibes from a crappy review."

"You haven't made it until you receive at least one of those."

I studied him. "How many crappy reviews have you received?"

"Enough. Not everyone shares my passion for sea lions. One student review said I drone on and on about them."

I grinned. "Well, you sorta do."

Ethan shook his head. "I think it's best you go back to your own desk now. I've got sea lion work to do."

"Only if you promise to do it quietly." I giggled and vacated his chair.

Who would have thought I'd be laughing after another visit from Max? Max's appearance may have ignited fear in me, but Ethan's words had dispelled it enough to make me laugh. He said I was strong, and with him by my side, I felt that way.

CHAPTER TWENTY-EIGHT

Ethan

DEALING with Max had taken all the energy out of me. It was like dealing with my father. He didn't understand the word no. He'd tried to visit us when we went to live with our grandparents. Gran and Gramps had refused. I remember listening to the conversation from the other side of the door. It sounded like he was never going to give up. But Gramps outlasted him.

Lily and Jack were sitting on the porch, watching me as I approached. I dropped into a chair next to them. Jasmine had gone to check on the kids.

"Looks like you've had one of those days," Jack said.

"Yeah. Max turned up."

Jack and Lily glanced at each other.

"Is Jasmine OK?" Lily asked.

"Yeah. Frustrated, but OK."

"I didn't even see him," Jack said. "Not much of a look-out, am I?"

"What did he want?" Lily asked.

"To see the kids. Jasmine said no. She told him to contact her solicitor."

Jack nodded. "Good girl."

"He's not going to give up."

"Has Jasmine contacted the police yet?"

"The sergeant said there's nothing he can do. We just need to keep him up to date. If Max becomes violent in any way, he'll come right out."

"That's no help," Lily said, clenching her hands together.

"What about his parole officer? Have the police contacted him?"

"The sergeant said the parole officer would have a word to Max. Let him know his actions aren't wise."

Jack grunted. I knew how he felt. It was like something had to happen before anyone would act. What good would that do?

"Is Jasmine going to tell the kids?"

"She's torn. She doesn't want them to be scared. But they need to be aware."

It was such a hard choice. Kids were resilient, but constantly being on alert was unhealthy for them. That was all my young life had been.

I stood. "Anyway, I thought I'd keep you up to date."

"Let us know if you need anything," Jack said.

"I will." I walked down the stairs and headed home.

I hated that Max had invaded Jasmine's peaceful life. She and the children had made a happy life without him. Now it was all at risk. I shouldn't compare Max to my father. Max had done horrible things but maybe he'd changed. Maybe he wasn't a narcissistic asshole anymore. But I didn't think so. He'd never apologised for what he'd done. He played it like he was the victim. He'd tried to play me that first night we'd met. If he had changed, he would have contacted the lawyer and started going through the correct channels.

I also hated that our workplace wasn't Max-free. Our office had been ours, just Jasmine's and mine. That was ridiculous. There was no Jasmine and me. We were all show.

I neared the house. Rose was calling out for Timmy, her voice high. She walked down the porch stairs, calling his name and searching the garden.

"Rose?" I sped up to reach her side, and she looked up at me with tears welling in her eyes.

"Ethan, Timmy's gone."

CHAPTER TWENTY-NINE

Jasmine

Ethan strode into the house and threw his bag on the couch. "Where have you looked?" he asked with no preamble.

"Inside. Bailey's looking again."

He swivelled back to the front door. "I'll do a door knock."

My pulse beat erratically. I caught up to him and grabbed his arm. "You don't think Max took him, do you?"

Ethan turned to face me and placed his hands on my upper arms. "Timmy can be very quick. He could have got out when we left this morning."

"Surely we would have noticed."

Ethan gave my arms a firm rub. "Let's try to find him before we jump to conclusions."

"OK."

It made sense. At least one of us was calm under pressure.

"I'm going to start next door and work my way down. Go and help Rose."

Did he mean help her or supervise her to make sure she was safe? It didn't matter. Helping her would serve both purposes.

I went outside and started searching with Rose. It could be a coincidence that Timmy had gone missing the day Max showed up again. Ethan was right. Timmy liked to run out the door with us. Maybe we hadn't noticed him this morning. And really, would Max stoop that low? Maybe if he was here to save the day and rescuing the cat would make him look good. But he wasn't here.

Ethan was walking through the house next door calling for Timmy. His footsteps and voice bounced off the walls of the empty rooms. He'd not even given a second thought to helping. If it were Max in the same situation, he would have grumbled about the stupid fucking cat.

If Ethan caring for us as a family was just a front, he was putting up a good one. Maybe I was reading too much into this. For the first time in years, I was uncertain, scared. And Ethan was offering us security. That's all it was. The way I reacted to his touch and the way he looked at me was a product of that.

Ethan came out of the house. He spotted me and shook his head before moving on to the next house. Rose and I had exhausted searching the yard and under the house.

Bailey came out the front door. "He's not inside."

Rose's eyes filled with tears. "Where is he, Mummy?"

I took her hand. "Let's check the yard next door. Maybe he's there."

The three of us made our way there and started searching. If Timmy was here, he would have come by now. He always came when the kids called. I scanned the beach. I doubt he'd go there.

"Look who I found," Ethan said, coming towards us with Timmy in hand.

Rose ran to him, took Timmy in her arms, and smooched and admonished him at the same time.

"Where was he?" Bailey asked, giving Timmy a pat.

"He was locked in the garage two houses down. He must have been there all afternoon. The people said they got home and parked a little after lunch."

"Oh, poor Timmy," Rose cooed. "You must be hungry." She carried him into the house and straight to his food bowl in the laundry.

"Thank you for your help," I said to Ethan.

"No problem."

"I'm sorry you didn't get to go out in the boat this afternoon."

"I can go tomorrow."

Bailey spun to face us. "We can still go. There's time before dinner." He moved from foot to foot, raising his eyebrows in invitation.

Ethan laughed. "Don't you have homework to do?"

"Nah, school's nearly finished. We don't get homework anymore."

Ethan turned his attention to me and lifted his shoulder. I sighed. I wasn't going to win this one. "Rose," I called out. "Do you want to go for a swim with the sea lions?"

She appeared in the laundry doorway almost instantly. "What about Timmy?"

"I think he's had enough adventure for one day," I said.

I ANCHORED THE BOAT, and the kids made their way to the stairs. The water was calm, lapping softly against the hull. Clouds flitted across the sky, casting shadows in the water.

"Stay close, this won't be a long swim," I said.

They nodded and jumped into the water. Rose squealed. The sea lions on shore perked up.

Ethan peeled his t-shirt off. His golden, tanned skin glowed. How did someone who did no exercise except when he was out here and ate like a king look like that? Why couldn't he have a dad bod?

My eyes raked over his chest, lower still, to the small trail of hair just above his shorts. I swallowed, nearly choking. I corrected my gaze to Ethan's eyes which were watching me.

Fuck. Just act normal.

If blushing like a red sunset was normal, I was nailing it.

"Aren't you going to work?" I managed to ask. As if it wasn't already obvious. I mean everyone took their shirt off to work, didn't they?

"No. I thought a swim would be a good way to end the day."

I nodded. "Good plan."

"Are you coming in?"

"Sure."

It would be a good way to cool off. And keep myself distracted. From him. I pulled my dress off and followed him down the stairs in my swim shorts and crop top. Before I could swim away to get some distance, Ethan pointed to the children. "Look, the injured sea lion is playing with them."

Sure enough, the sea lion was swimming circles around them and then darting off for them to follow.

"At least there are two humans in the world he likes," I said.

"And you," Ethan said. "He's never as wary with you as he is me."

A sea lion darted between us, pushing us apart. Ethan chuckled and dove down to the sand after it. I swam in the opposite direction, smiling to myself. Ethan was right. This was a good end to the day. Spending time with the people you loved, or *liked* in Ethan's case, was never a bad thing.

CHAPTER THIRTY

Ethan

I SAT at the small desk in my room, sending the notes from my iPad to my laptop. I had a lot that I needed to sort through to decide what would be appropriate for my report. It was hard to tell what would be valuable as my research continued and my thought processes shifted. Rose and Bailey were in the living area having one of their discussions. I tried to drown out their voices.

"Rose, leave him alone," Bailey said.

"I don't want him to miss out on decorating."

I smiled to myself even though I should have been concentrating on the words in front of me. Rose thought Timmy needed to be involved in everything. And Timmy often was, whether he wanted to be or not.

"I'm sure he's decorated a million times."

I cocked my head. The only thing Timmy decorated was his litter box.

"But he hasn't decorated with us. I'm going to get him."

Loud footsteps approached my room in a rush. Rose came bursting in and slid to a stop next to me. "Ethan, it's time to put up the Christmas tree."

I closed my laptop. There was no way I was going to get any more work done today. I went out into the living room with Rose. Bailey shook his head at her, but couldn't contain his grin. Jasmine was nowhere to be seen.

"Where's your mom?"

"Getting the Christmas tree," Rose said.

Bailey headed to the laundry. "The box is up in the roof space."

There was no attic in this house. What did he mean? I went into the laundry. There was a ladder in the middle of the room, leading to a hole in the ceiling. Bailey pointed up to it.

"We go through the manhole to store things up there that we don't use much."

Jasmine's face appeared. "I'm going to lower down the Christmas boxes. Can you grab them please, Bails?"

"Yep."

The boxes were tied in rope. Attached to it was another length of rope which Jasmine used to lower the box down. She repeated the process three times while I helped Bailey retrieve the boxes and take them to the living area.

"Can you hold the ladder steady while I climb down, please?" Jasmine asked me.

I glanced between the ladder, Jasmine in the manhole and the floor. This didn't look safe at all. My heart raced. Surely she didn't do this with just her and the kids. What if something went wrong?

"Ethan?"

"Sorry, yes."

I strode over to the ladder and held it firm. Jasmine's

face disappeared, then her long legs appeared and her feet found the rungs. She descended slowly. The ladder moved slightly, and I gripped onto it. There was no way Jasmine was falling on my watch. Lower she came until her feet were equal with my face. Then her shapely calves. Her curvy butt.

Her back brushed against me. She may have been closer to the floor, but I wasn't letting go of that ladder until her feet hit the ground. When she reached the floor, she was encircled in my arms. Safe. And trapped. I took a breath in. The dust on her skin almost overpowered the citrus scent of her hair. I needed to move out of her way. I let go of the ladder and stepped back at the same time she turned around and walked into me. A gush of air left my lungs.

She laughed. It was a joyous sound that I would forever associate with Christmas. Her brown eyes glowed with warmth. Crap. I needed to stop staring.

"Sorry," I said, moving out of her way.

"I see the kids roped you into helping with the tree."

"Rose didn't leave me much choice."

"You don't have to help if you are busy with your work."

My work or decorating the tree with them...any other time I would have chosen my work. But something about this family invited me to join in any chance I got. That wasn't a good idea. My being a part of their close-knit family was supposed to be fake.

"Decorating sounds like fun," I said, walking to the living room. So much for keeping my distance.

Rose and Bailey had pulled the tree out of the box and were assembling it. Rose had the smaller top part and Bailey the bottom. I stood and watched not knowing what they needed me to do.

"Ethan, can you help us join the tree together? It's really hard," Rose said.

I took the top half of the tree from Rose. Bailey held the bottom half steady while I tried to join the trunk together. It took a bit of force but was worth the work. When the tree stood tall and ready for decorating, Rose's face shone with delight.

I helped with the baubles, tinsel, and lights. Then Rose stood before us with the angel. She glanced between Jasmine and me then held it out.

"You and Mum can put the angel on this year."

I lost the ability to speak. Rose placed the Angel in my hand, and I walked toward the tree with Jasmine. She took hold of it and we lifted it onto the tree together. I stole a glance at her, at the serene smile on her face. When she made eye contact with me, it was like everything else disappeared for that miniscule moment.

Rose hugged us both and said, "It's perfect."

I stepped away and nodded, still unable to formulate words. But perfect about summed it up.

CHAPTER THIRTY-ONE

Jasmine

I sat out the front of the shop with Lily and Sara while the kids played on the beach. The sea breeze made today's heat bearable. This heat wave had lasted for three days. The days were stifling and swimming was a constant relief.

"Ethan came to the shop yesterday for bananas," Lily said. "He said he was making dessert for you all."

"Oooh that's sweet," Sara said, twirling her blonde plait.

"He made us all banana splits. The kids loved them."

It was the best banana split I'd ever had. But I guessed it was like sandwiches, they always tasted better when someone else made them.

"Where's Ethan today?" Sara asked.

Why did she want to know?

"Working on his report at the office. He said it was easier to use two screens."

"That makes sense," Lily said. "He told Jack the other day that Bailey was helping him by reading out figures and noticed that something looked strange. They looked at the data together and Ethan realised he'd written a number down wrong."

I couldn't believe Ethan told Jack about it. I can still remember Bailey glowing when Ethan told him it was a good pick up.

Sara nodded and smiled. "He told me about it too."

Ethan hadn't told me he'd seen Sara. I glanced at her sideways. "When did you see Ethan?"

"The other day."

"What other day?"

"Why do you care?"

"I was just curious." I leant back in my chair.

"Nothing more, just curious?" Lily asked with a smirk.

I huffed. "Everyone knows everything in this town, but I didn't know that he'd seen Sara. I was curious. That's all."

"Uh-huh."

I ignored her and looked at Sara, inviting her to tell me more, like maybe why Ethan had visited her.

"Anyway, he was telling me how Bailey was smart enough to pick up that mistake and then he was telling me about Rose and how he loves the new words she comes up with."

I loved it too.

"I took credit for that. I told him she hated learning her sight words at school, so I made a deal with her—for every ten she learnt off by heart I would give her a bigger, more impressive word to learn."

She took the credit? It wasn't just her. I was part of the deal too. I'd persevered with Rose day after day, week after week. I bought her book after book about mermaids until she was the best reader in her year. Just because Sara came up with the idea didn't mean she should get *all* the credit.

Wait, what did it even matter who got the credit?

Normally, I celebrated Sara for what she helped us achieve. And now I wasn't? It was all of us who contributed, and especially Rose who did the hard work and fell in love with words. The fact that Ethan noticed and appreciated it made me feel all warm inside. Max wouldn't have appreciated Bailey pointing out a mistake. And he wouldn't have appreciated Rose and her aptitude for being the centre of attention.

"Jasmine?" Lily said.

I glanced between Sara and Lily. What question or comment had I missed?

"Have you bought Ethan a Christmas present?"

"I got him something small. I didn't want anything big or heavy because he has to take it all the way back to the States." My stomach dropped and weight lingered there.

"What did you get him?"

"I'm not telling you. You can't keep a secret to save yourself Mrs Did the Coffee Smell Good."

I looked down at my hands. Why did the realisation that Ethan would be leaving make me a little sad? Friends leave all the time. And that's all we were. He was here for his research, and we were living together, pretending to be more than we were to protect the children.

CHAPTER THIRTY-TWO

Ethan

I took Jasmine's hand as we headed to the weekly bonfire together. Hers was relaxed in mine as if it was natural for us. But it wasn't. It was only for show.

We all fit into an easy routine together. I felt closer to them than I had been to anyone in a long time. This was dangerous ground. What if I let myself go and the true me came out? What if I hurt them like Max had or I turned into my dad? Being close to people could make you think you had some sort of ownership over them, that they should bend to your will. I needed to be on guard, watch my actions. I couldn't get distance even if I wanted to. If the house next door was finished just after Christmas like promised, I still couldn't move out. I was trapped in this pleasure I'd created for myself.

"You're quiet," Jasmine said.

"Just thinking."

"About?"

What was I going to tell her? Perhaps a little of the truth

wouldn't hurt. No, I couldn't. Audrey knew the truth and had turned it against me.

Jasmine stopped and twisted towards me. The kids kept walking. They weren't going to save me. Jasmine searched my eyes.

"Does it ever get hard hiding yourself all the time?"

Straight to the crux of it. She wasn't accusing or belittling. Her voice was gentle. She saw me like no one ever had. There was no point hiding because she already knew. Somehow.

"I learned to do it from a young age."

"Because of your father?"

I took a deep breath. "Yes."

"You know our house, our family is a safe zone where we share without fear of retribution."

"I know." I'd witnessed it many times.

"Would you like to share with me now?"

I shifted from foot to foot. What was I going to say? I'd preferred to say nothing. Why did I do this to myself? I was the only one to blame here for putting myself in this position. But Jasmine shared with me. I should share with her too. Shouldn't I?

I'm scared was a big statement. I couldn't say the words. "I worry that if I let go of this facade, I might be just like my father underneath." Oh God, I'd said it. I looked down at my feet. It was easier than watching her reaction. So much for being on guard. I couldn't trust myself around her, telling her things I shouldn't. But why did I? Was I trying to sway her feelings toward me?

She squeezed my hands. "Ethan."

I forced myself to meet her gaze.

"I would tell you if I thought that was the case."

We began walking again. She didn't question me

further, instead allowing me time to process. This woman who had been so damn tough on me at the start had insight I'd never experienced before. I smiled to myself. It must have infuriated her that I never spoke back.

"Well, look at you two," Jack said. "You look like you've been sharing more than just lustful stares."

He didn't just say that, did he? What the fuck? My head whipped around to see if anyone had heard.

Jasmine shook her head. "Seriously, Jack, you need to stop reading those romance novels. Your imagination is running wild."

He waggled his eyebrows. "I don't need romance novels."

"Maybe a psychiatrist then."

Jasmine walked off, and I followed, Jack chuckling behind us.

We sat next to Lily. The kids were much more relaxed tonight, less on edge than they had been the week before. Jasmine's decision not to tell them about Max's last visit had been a good one. I still wasn't sure if my opening up, even if a tiny bit to Jasmine, was a good decision. But it was done now. The use of my name drew my attention to the conversation.

Jasmine glanced at me. "He's doing a six-month research project on the sea lion population here."

"Oh really, what type of research?" one camper asked.

Before I could. reply, Jasmine said, "He's recording data about their numbers, feeding, breeding, where they travel. It's very in-depth."

Was that pride in her voice? Audrey had never been interested in anything I did. Warmth spread through me.

"What are you hoping to find?" another camper asked.

Jasmine didn't answer this time, but she smiled at me, inviting me to speak.

"Sea lion populations are decreasing around the world. I'm hoping to learn more about their behaviours in the wild. Get an understanding of what may be causing it."

"You're American?" someone asked. "What made you come all the way to Haven Bay?"

"The sea lions."

"Not love?" an elderly woman asked.

Jasmine and I shared a look.

"Love was the furthest thing from my mind when I came here," I admitted.

The elderly woman smiled a knowing smile. "And now that seems to have changed."

My throat constricted. Love was a big word. I had deeper feelings for Jasmine than I'd felt in a long time. But it wasn't love. More like a deep mutual respect.

Sara arrived at that moment with the fish and chips, saving me from having to reply. When she handed Lily her food, she whispered something in her ear. They both stole a glance at Jasmine and me and smiled. I shifted in my seat. These people and this town were too much sometimes. I suspected they knew more about Jasmine and me than we ourselves did.

CHAPTER THIRTY-THREE

Jasmine

I WALKED DOWN to the water's edge, leaving the frivolity around the bonfire behind. The ocean stretched out before me, an expanse bigger than I could imagine. Ethan lived at the edge of another ocean and in four months' time he'd be returning to it.

Haven Bay was our haven, the kids and mine. We'd been safe here for years. Ethan had now become our haven too. But he would be leaving. The kids would be heartbroken when he left. They'd become attached to him in such a short time. It surprised me.

"Your turn," Ethan said, appearing beside me. Where did he come from?

"For what?"

"To share your thoughts."

What was I going to tell him? That I'd been thinking about him leaving? I deserved this; I'd called him out earlier. How the tables had turned.

I faced him. The wind picked at the tendrils of my hair,

and Ethan reached out, moving it out of my face. His fingers lingered on my skin, a warm caress that heated my insides. His gaze roamed my face. Everything inside me was pulled toward him like a magnet, but I stood firm. My fingers itched to touch him, to feel him. I didn't let them. It took all my power to keep my hands by my side.

His hand dropped. "Your turn," he said, his voice husky.

Hot damn. That sent my female parts into a frenzy. This was nuts. I took a tiny step back to save my dignity.

"This is our haven, Ethan. Where we feel safe. You make us feel safe too."

What the hell did I say that for? Would he retreat? Would he deflect?

He cupped my cheek. I could have melted into a puddle.

"Good."

Good? Is that all he had for me? His hand retracted like he'd suddenly felt pain. I longed for it to return.

His eyes widened. "Good," he repeated, nodding. Then he turned and walked away.

I stared at his retreating back, then spun around and stared at the water.

Havens aren't always safe.

I NEEDED to speak to Lily. These feelings I was having didn't make sense. Last night was too much to bear on my own.

I walked into the store.

"Jasmine, darling," Jack said in a jaunty voice.

I strode past him, holding up my hand. "Don't start."

A smart quip didn't follow.

I found Lily in the lounge area out the back, watching a house renovation show. I slumped down in the armchair and stared at the television. Lily did the same.

"Are you here to talk about last night?" she asked.

"Maybe." My determination had left me. I continued staring at the TV.

"Would you like me to start for you?"

I sighed. This was so stupid. My feelings were irrational.

"You're confused about your feelings for Ethan."

I stood and started pacing. "I don't know what I'm feeling. I mean I like him. Anyone would like him. He's nice." I stopped and shook my hands. No, staying still was no good. "Maybe it's because we live together and work together. Being so close is mixing things up." I paused. Even my thoughts weren't making sense. "And then he pulls this protector thing. And he makes me feel protected. But maybe it's just because I'm scared. And his knight in shining armour act got me when I was at my most vulnerable." I sat back in the chair. "But what's even the point of having feelings when he's only here for six months?" I looked at Lily, imploring her to understand. "And the kids. God, the kids adore him. I think they do. Oh shit, I don't know."

Lily gave me a smile. "That's a lot to digest."

I ran my hand over my face, touched the place he'd lain his palm. "And I think I want him to kiss me."

I didn't think I wanted him to. I knew I wanted him to. Fuck.

"Maybe you should let him."

"What?"

"You should let him kiss you."

"Who even says he wants to?"

Lily turned her full body to me. "Even blind Freddy can see the man wants to kiss you."

"And then what?"

Lily let out a quiet laugh. "You have two children; I don't think I need to tell you then what."

"Lily."

"OK. OK. You and Ethan were getting closer before Max showed up. Even after he got his boat licence, you would go out with him to do his research."

"It's easier and safer with two people."

She held up her hand. "And this protector thing is not for show. He had nothing to gain that night with Rose and the storm."

"I didn't mean it was just for show. I meant... I don't know what I meant."

"Stop overthinking everything. What will be will be." She shrugged. "Jack proposed to me the day we met. I could have over analysed it. Instead, I said yes."

"Not everyone is you and Jack."

"Not everyone is you and Ethan."

"Are you two OK back there?" Jack called out.

"Just talking about Sex on Legs," Lily replied.

"They mean you," Jack said, quieter this time.

Ethan was here?

I nearly fell off my seat. Lily laughed so hard she was crying.

CHAPTER THIRTY-FOUR

Ethan

I LOOKED at Jack with wide eyes. "They're talking about what?"

"Sex on Legs, you."

My brow furrowed. Jack chuckled and grabbed his phone. He typed something in and turned the phone to me. Pictures and pictures of me stared back at me. He clicked on one of the photos to make it larger. I was standing there in a wetsuit that was pulled down to my hips.

"Sex on Legs," Jack said.

I blushed. "What do you suppose they're talking about?"

"Perhaps the same thing you were coming to talk about."

I looked out the window at the kids playing on the beach, Timmy running between them. I didn't know exactly what I had come in to talk about.

"You may want to spit it out before they come out," Jack said.

I turned my attention back to him. "Jasmine."

Jack nodded, encouraging me to continue. When I didn't, he said, "You've been getting close."

There was the opening that I needed. "Yeah, but I don't know if it's because we're pretending."

"Are you pretending to like her?"

"No."

"Well, that's a start."

I shrugged.

"Let me tell you what I've seen. I've seen Jasmine, who doesn't trust many people, put her trust in you. I've seen her look at you like kids look at ice cream and I've seen you look at her like ice cream covered in chocolate topping."

I laughed. "I'm not good at relationships."

"Maybe because it wasn't with Jasmine."

"I'm only here for six months."

"Well, don't waste them then."

He made it sound so easy. Opening up was not easy. Being vulnerable was not easy. I was not easy.

Jasmine and Lily came out of an aisle. My insides were floating like when doing a deep dive. I needed to anchor myself. I glanced at Jasmine. She gave me a small smile, securing me like a dive line.

"Well, off you go, we've got the kids for the afternoon," Jack said.

"What?" Jasmine and I said in unison.

"We're taking them into Somewhere Bay for ice cream." Before either of us could say a word, he strode to the front door, flung it open and yelled, "Who wants ice cream?"

"Me," Rose and Bailey answered.

"Go get ready then," Jack said.

I carried Timmy while the kids ran ahead to get

changed. Jasmine walked beside me. We were both silent. This wasn't awkward at all.

"Sex on Legs, huh?" I gave her a smirk and waited for her reaction.

She kept her eyes straight ahead. "Lily's name for you."

"Not yours?"

She blushed. "I may have used it once or twice."

"I'll have to think of a pet name for you."

"Please don't."

"It only seems fair." I grinned as I gave her a nudge.

She rolled her eyes.

My mind wandered to another bonfire night and Lily commenting about coffee in her own little devious way. "Has that got something to do with the coffee smell Lily was talking about?"

Jasmine blushed crimson. "No. I told her you smell better than coffee."

It was my turn for my face to turn red.

"What shall we do for the rest of the day?" I snapped my head back to the front. There were lots of things I'd like to do with Jasmine—clothed, naked, or anything in between. But moving from pretending to real needed to come first. If that's what she wanted.

"How about a boat trip to Seclusion Bay for a picnic and swim?"

"Sounds great."

The kids were waiting at the door for us. This having to lock the door all the time was frustrating, but we needed to do it to keep safe.

"Go and get changed and we'll walk you to the shop," Jasmine said, unlocking the door.

"I'll get some lunch packed." I put Timmy down and went into the kitchen.

The kids were back in no time. Jasmine soon followed in a summer dress, her bikini straps poking out. My pulse quickened as I remembered the last time I'd seen her in swimwear—her short swim shorts and crop top accentuating her curves.

"I'll finish off. Can you grab some towels after you get dressed, please?" she asked.

"Sure can."

The kids watched me as if to hurry me along.

"The ice cream won't run out if Ethan takes a few minutes," she said.

I laughed. "I'll be quick."

Ten minutes later, after we'd dropped the kids off, we headed to the boat. "Do you want me to drive?" I asked.

"That would be nice." There she went relinquishing power again. A sign of trust, just like Jack had said.

We stood next to each other, quiet except when Jasmine was giving directions. Heat emanated off her as her arm pressed against mine. And we were alone, together, on purpose. I tightened my hand on the steering wheel.

We rounded the point into a cove, and I sucked a breath in. Beautiful white sand formed a semi-circle. The clear water changed from a deep turquoise to aquamarine the closer it got to shore. I stopped the boat.

"Wow."

"Beautiful, isn't it?" Jasmine smiled up at me with her full lips. Her warm brown eyes had me spellbound.

I nodded, not trusting myself to speak.

"Shall we swim first?" she asked.

"Sure." I dropped the anchor.

She turned toward the stern and lifted her dress off, revealing the remainder of her tanned legs. Her bikini wasn't the one she normally wore—no shorts and crop top.

The tropical print material was cut high, showing off her legs and shapely butt even more than her swim shorts had. More of her skin was revealed than I'd ever seen. It wasn't as tanned as the rest of her smooth, glowing skin. If she turned around—

I gulped. I shouldn't be watching her every movement like I was an ogling male sea lion ready to prove my genetic value. I concentrated instead on taking my tank top off and following her to the stairs, looking anywhere but at her and her graceful movement. I wasn't a sexed-up sea lion who couldn't control my hormones.

Luckily, we weren't at North Baker Beach, the nudist beach in San Francisco. I'd probably be told to leave because I was staring too much.

Jasmine jumped into the water and swam away. She turned and watched me, and every inch of my skin sparked to life. I didn't shy away from her open gaze. I didn't feel like I needed to hide. As I stepped onto the bottom step, I felt courage I'd never experienced before.

CHAPTER THIRTY-FIVE

Jasmine

I CAUGHT Ethan's eye as he stood on the bottom stair. He gave me that smile that captured my heart. No wonder women everywhere fawned over him. I kept my gaze on his instead of raking them over his body. It took all my determination to do so. I didn't want to treat him like sex on legs. Although, it surprised me that he had not been completely uncomfortable with the term. Especially after his reaction at his first wetsuit demonstration.

He jumped in and swam to me. My body was on full alert. It was hot regardless of the water surrounding me. If he touched me, would the water sizzle? I took a deep breath. And if he kissed me? I needed to stop this train of thought. I submerged my head, breaking the eye contact.

"Let's swim close to shore so we can take in the view from there," I said when I popped up. Anything was better than my wild thoughts.

I didn't wait for his answer. Ethan matched my leisurely strokes and soon my feet could reach the bottom. Ethan stood beside me surveying the view. We were in our own secluded paradise, surrounded by white sand and calm water that stretched out to the ocean beyond.

Ethan redirected his gaze toward me. "It's beautiful, like you."

My heart rate picked up.

The small waves lifted us, taking my feet off the ground. He gently clasped my waist, keeping us tethered together. I cupped the side of his face and ran my thumb over his lips. His breath faltered. His eyes searched mine before he pulled me closer. His large hands were gentle and firm as he held me against him.

I wound my fingers into his thick hair and pulled his head closer. His soft breath mixed with mine. Our lips touched. My insides were nothingness, a gaping emptiness, full of want and urgency. For him. He coaxed my lips open. Saltiness slipped over my taste buds. Pleasant and satisfying.

Our bodies fused together. Nothing moved but our lips and tongues. Our breath was harsh as we chased the endorphins, catching them one by one. He caught my soft moans the same way. And then my heart.

Ethan's lips slowed, and he pulled away. My heart thumped in my chest. His teeth gently pulled at my lip as we separated.

"That was better than the view," he breathed.

I nodded. I had no words. That was the best kiss I'd ever had. And I wanted another and another.

Was this even a good idea? I didn't care. For once, I didn't need to be in control.

CHAPTER THIRTY-SIX

Ethan

I LAY in bed thinking about the day, the boat ride, the swim, the kiss. I'd started the day confused and as I lay there my mind showed me I still was. I'd opened up to her with fear in my heart. And the fear was still there. But not the same as it once had been. I wasn't scared about being judged or that she would be calculating and use it against me in the future.

I was scared that piece by piece I would unravel and then what was left would show an empty soul. I thought about every conversation we'd had and every time I divulged something new...it had been both a relief and a burden. Because I didn't understand why I was doing it.

I breathed in deeply and let it out slowly. I needed to situate myself. I was in bed. The sound of small waves lapping against the shore was constant. The lack of streetlights meant the only light came from the moon. I took another deep breath.

Kissing Jasmine had been better than I could have imagined. It was like I was alive for the first time in a long time.

A fire had been stoked. A fire could be coaxed gently or it could erupt. I needed to keep it at the lower level. I needed to not lose myself completely.

I shook my head. I needed not to think about the fear of losing myself, but to enjoy the memory of the kiss. And enjoy Jasmine for all she was. That kiss had been fantastic.

I'd sort of been in a daze after it. Our afternoon had been just like any other afternoon when the kids got home. Was she lying in her bed now, two doors away, thinking about it? Would the morning be weird? Would she regret it?

JASMINE SMILED at me as I entered the kitchen, gesturing to a cup on the bench. "Made your coffee for you."

"Thanks."

As I took the cup, I inhaled the strong aroma. Jasmine making a coffee for me was unexpected. I was usually the one making coffee. My stomach lifted. It may have been a small gesture, but it showed me what it was like to be cared for. I'd never really had that before from someone other than family.

"It's not such a rush in the morning now the kids are on holidays, so I have more time."

I grinned. "Did you make my breakfast too?"

She gave me a friendly nudge. "Don't push your luck."

"Does that mean a kiss is off the table too?" I turned her toward me. "It would make a great start to the morning."

What the hell was I doing? I had no idea if Jasmine regretted the kiss or not. Maybe the coffee was her way of letting me down gently. She glanced in the direction of the kids' bedroom. They were awake. I could hear Rose talking to Timmy.

Jasmine clasped the back of my neck and tilted her head up to mine. Our lips met for a moment, long enough for me to appreciate the softness of hers. She pulled away and ran her tongue across her lips just as Rose came running into the kitchen. So maybe the kiss wasn't a once off.

This was madness. And I was embracing it.

CHAPTER THIRTY-SEVEN

Jasmine

THIS MORNING's kiss had my insides humming. I smiled as Ethan and I approached the meeting point and greeted our guests. The smile was less perfunctory than usual. I felt it on the inside, like my lips weren't the only thing that was lifted.

I began telling them what their morning with the sea lions would be like. My gaze landed on a face I'd rather not see—Max. My smile died and I paused mid-sentence. Ethan stopped what he was doing and looked in Max's direction, his jaw hardening.

I shook my head and continued. "The water temperature today is around twenty degrees Celsius. You can opt to swim with or without a wetsuit. Ethan will demonstrate how to put one on."

Ethan went through his presentation without a hitch. My eyes darted between him and Max. There was no enjoying the view today. Max certainly wasn't. His cold eyes said more than his rigid shoulders.

As the guests went to put on their wetsuits, I busied myself with packing the leftovers. Ethan stayed close, his eyes darting between me and Max. Max hadn't moved.

Could the man not understand one simple fucking instruction? Contact the solicitor. But of course, he wouldn't do that. Once family court mediation started and the kids needed to talk to a psychologist it would be revealed how shitty a person he was. Of course, they could possibly be swayed by his charm, but maybe not. That wasn't a risk he'd want to take. He would think it easier to influence me than a trained professional. After all, he'd done it for ten years.

I guided the guests onto the boat. Ethan took up the rear. Max made sure he was right behind me and then sat as close as he could to the steering wheel. As I drove off, I rolled my shoulders, trying to relax them.

I concentrated on Ethan's voice as he spoke about the sea lions and tried not to think of Max's eyes boring into my back. What was he even doing here, anyway? Did he think stalking was going to get him anywhere?

It was the first day of the school holidays. He must have known that. And that was exactly why he was here. He would be trying to see the kids by accident, on purpose. The mobile phone was useless, so I couldn't let Jack and Lily know he was here and to look out for him when we got back to shore. I could use the radio, but I didn't want the guests to know there was some sort of problem. At least when he was on the boat, he was nowhere near them.

I stopped the boat and anchored it while Ethan gave the final instructions. Then the guests made their way into the water. Except for Max.

"Are you going in?" I asked.

Ethan stood at the stern, watching the swimmers.

"No. I prefer the company up here." He sent a pointed look in Ethan's direction.

"Fine, sit there then. I've got a job to do."

I positioned myself so my back wasn't to him, but I could still see the swimmers. Sea lions swam amongst them, getting closer, circling and diving.

"I can see what you like about him. He puts on a good show with the wetsuit."

I ignored him. As did Ethan. He was tense though. I saw it in his stance.

Was it Max that had posted that review and signed it Mr R? R for Mr Reynard? It was something he would do. He liked to undermine people.

A swimmer was following a sea lion, getting further and further away from the boat. Ethan sounded the hand-held horn and ushered the swimmer back.

"He's not much more than that though," Max said loud enough just for me to hear.

For fuck's sake, what was his problem? Why couldn't he leave us alone? Ethan was more than just his body or an interest in sea lions. He was kind and thoughtful. Not only that, he had confidence in me. He always let me handle situations myself and stepped in only if needed.

"The kids are home today. Maybe we can see them when we go back."

I watched the swimmers, sneaking a look at Ethan. He hadn't changed his posture. I didn't know what was worse—Max speaking or the long drawn-out silence in between.

"Have you spoken to them about me?"

I didn't want to engage with Max. But with every word he spoke, it was harder not to. I clenched my teeth and took a deep breath through my nose, reminding myself that getting angry with him would serve no purpose. Telling him what I thought would serve no purpose. He wanted me to respond, and I would do everything in my power not to. He wouldn't listen anyway.

"I'm here. They're here. What would it hurt to see them?"

A middle-aged man came back to the boat. Before Ethan helped him onto the boat, I turned to Max. "Talk to my solicitor."

Max scowled.

The swimmer was gushing. "That was fantastic. I could do this every day."

Ethan smiled at him. "The sea lion that was swimming with you is a male juvenile."

"How do you know?"

"I recognise him. Also, juveniles are small like the females and grey on top with a cream underbelly. But if I didn't know I could read his tag number. Did you notice he had a tag on his fin?"

"One on each side."

"The tag number starts with H B to show that it was first tagged in Haven Bay. Then it is followed by four digits. That's its unique number. We can look it up in a database."

The man started to take his wetsuit off.

"We prefer to take the wetsuits off when we get back. That way we don't have them lying all over the boat causing a trip hazard."

"No worries."

More and more swimmers returned, their faces aglow from their experience. On the ride back, Ethan shared a bit about his research. I noted that he didn't mention it was a six-month project like he normally would. When we reached the jetty, Jack was standing at the end with two male police officers. I smiled to myself. Either Jack had seen Max or the kids had. And they'd done the smartest thing possible.

It was time for Max to be reminded that our life didn't involve him anymore.

CHAPTER THIRTY-EIGHT

Ethan

To SAY that I was pleased the police were here was an understatement. I was getting tired of Max... fast. He'd infiltrated every part of our life. Turning up to a tour where we had no option but to be polite and smile was a conniving and infuriating move.

Jasmine had done an amazing job. She'd hardly uttered a word until she told him to contact the solicitor. He didn't like that. He didn't like that he couldn't connect with her, which meant he couldn't sway her. His third arrival made me wonder if it was more Jasmine he was trying to connect with rather than the children. I thought he would have tried to see the kids on the sly, bypassing Jasmine altogether. Today would have been the prime opportunity. But it was her he kept making contact with.

Any person would understand that she wanted nothing to do with him. Any person *other* than Max. I just wanted to grab him and tell him to fuck off. I took a deep breath and willed calmness through my body. The police were here now. Surely, they would do something. Would it be enough?

We escorted the guests off. The police pulled Max to the side while Jasmine and I went through the normal routine with our guests. I didn't like that idea. It gave him time to construct the narrative he wanted. At least Jack was there.

When we finished with the last guest, we headed over to the police.

"Jasmine, Ethan," the older officer said. "Jack called us about Mr Reynard."

Jasmine considered them both. I knew she was on first-name terms with them. It was a ranger thing and a small-town thing.

"I've told Max repeatedly that if he wants to see the children he needs to speak to my solicitor."

The policeman turned to Max.

"It's been five years, officer. I'm desperate to see my children."

Here we go. Playing the victim card. Now we would see how far Jasmine's relationship with the police would take her. The younger police officer shifted from foot to foot. The older one remained staunch.

"That may be the case. But papers we have on file state that Jasmine has full custody of the children and your visitation rights have been withheld."

"I wasn't aware of those papers, sir. As I'm sure you know, I've been tied up for the past five years."

Is that what we're going to call being in jail now?

The young officer watched the older one, scrutinising his every move.

"Yes, Mr Reynard. I'm aware of your circumstances." He glanced at Jasmine before returning his stern look to Max. "I will take your word that you were unaware of the court order. However, as of this moment, you are."

Max's jaw twitched.

"My advice to you is to contact a solicitor and not to come back here until the family court allows you access."

Twitch. Twitch.

"Thank you, officer. I will take that under advisement." Max turned his attention to us, but not before a sneaky glance at the young officer. He addressed Jasmine. "I'm sorry if I've upset you. I only wanted to see my children."

"You can see Bailey and Rose when the family court grants you permission."

Twitch. Twitch. Fucking twitch.

Max thanked the officers before walking away.

"Please contact us if he appears again," the older officer said. "We'll leave you to the rest of your day now."

They headed back to their car. While they were still in earshot, I heard the sergeant say, "You've got a lot to learn about the arseholes of this world. That man was lying out of his arse."

"Hopefully that deters him for a while," Jack said. He strolled away, leaving Jasmine and me alone.

She turned to me. "He'll be back."

"I know. His thinly disguised anger said it all."

"You saw it too. We'll need to keep the kids close."

I nodded. That man was ready to explode. I didn't want the kids to see it, but I didn't want them away from us either.

Jasmine looked down the road out of town. One way in. One way out. No escape if we needed it. If it came to it, I would protect her and the children with everything I had. I took her hand and led her along the sand.

"Was this what it was like with your father?" she asked.

I looked out at the water. This opening up thing was hard. "My father was emotionally coercive and physically abusive." That was a good start. Stating facts and not feelings was easier. "The abuse was mainly directed at Steve and me. I took the brunt of it though. Steve is younger than me. It was my job to protect him." Time and time again. I sighed. "My mother never learned. When she got cancer, people donated for her treatment. He took it all."

Her hand tightened. "That's terrible."

"He wore her down until she had no opinions of her own. She always took his side."

Jasmine shook her head. It would be hard for a mother like Jasmine to understand.

"Is that why you hide your feelings?"

My heart thumped. There was no hiding from her questions.

"I didn't do it because he wanted me to. I did it to save myself. I didn't want him to have power over me." I sighed. "When Audrey and I got married, I vowed not to be like my father. I let her do what she wanted, never argued, never tried to convince her of anything."

We stopped walking and sat at the end of the jetty.

"She was spoiled. And bored. In the end, she told me I was like my father, but my weapon was silence."

"It must have hurt to hear that."

"She knew those words would hurt." Why couldn't I stop myself from talking? They just kept flowing out of me. "She said me letting her do whatever she wanted showed that I didn't care about her or our relationship."

Jasmine rested her hand on my leg. "Do you think

maybe your silence has eaten away at you? Like first, you weren't allowed to share your opinion and then you were too scared to share your opinion?"

Was she talking about her experience with Max?

I nodded. "In my work life, I'm fine. No one can get hurt. What I say is based on science, not emotions." I ran my hand through my hair. "My personal life is different. I'm always worried that when I say something, it's for my own agenda."

Like now. I was telling her these things I kept hidden. Was I doing that so she would trust me? And what exactly was I going to do with that trust?

She turned to face me, tucking a leg under herself. "Do you tell me I'm a good mum for your own agenda?"

I shook my head. "It's because you are."

"Do you tell the children that I'm brave and strong for your own agenda?"

"No."

"Do you compliment and encourage the children for your own agenda?"

"No."

"Would your father have done any of those things?"

"The opposite. He always told my mom how bad a mother she was."

"See. You're not repeating your father's failures."

True. What she said was true. She made it sound logical, but could it be that easy? Being with her was easier than I had ever imagined. So much easier.

I smiled. "I did kiss you for my own agenda though."

"And what agenda was that?"

"This." I cupped the back of her head and pulled her toward me. Her lips were soft and supple, so willing they opened at the slightest touch. Her tongue swept across mine, sending a heated jolt through me. And damn if I wasn't going to take everything she was going to give.

My hands ached to touch her curves, to feel them and memorise them. But not here, not where everyone could see. No, this kiss was a premise of what was to come.

I wanted to kiss Jasmine one hundred different ways in one hundred different places.

CHAPTER THIRTY-NINE

Jasmine

With the morning tour out of the way, we were heading to one of the campsites within the national park. The walking track needed to be checked to ensure it was in good condition and the bathrooms needed their routine clean. Bailey and Rose had been unusually quiet.

"Mum," Rose said from the backseat, "Why were the police here?"

Ethan glanced at me. We hadn't realised they'd seen or heard anything. "Your dad came on a tour today to ask if he can see you."

"I don't want to see him," Rose declared.

"I know, Rose. I have told him you and Bailey aren't ready."

"Then why does he keep coming?"

I glanced in the rearview mirror. Bailey was staring out the window, listening but not engaging. Ethan looked over his shoulder.

"The police have told him he needs to speak to a solicitor. Do you know what a solicitor is?" I asked.

Rose nodded. "They help with the law."

"That's right. Our solicitor will help make sure that your dad sees you only after the family court says he can, when you're ready."

"I don't want to see him. He's a bad person."

"I know."

Bailey was still quiet. What was he thinking about back there? Was he as scared as Rose? It wasn't good for him to bottle his feelings up.

We parked at the campground and hopped out of the car. There was a cleared area for tents and campers which surrounded a fire pit and a small amenities block.

"Bailey and I will clean the amenities. You can start out here," Ethan said.

I cocked my head. It was unusual for him to take charge like that. "Come on, Rose, let's make sure the area around the fire pit is clean. It will stop any accidental fires."

She skipped away and I followed. Ethan and Bailey went into the bathroom.

"You were quiet in the car," Ethan said, the sound travelling easily across the space.

Rose was singing to herself, clearing the area and paying no attention to the conversation I was listening to. I imagined Bailey shrugging.

"Do you want to see your dad?"

Silence. Was there a shrug or a shake of the head? Maybe a nod? Was my fear stopping him from having a relationship with Max?

"No. I hate him." Bailey's voice was quiet. "It was my fault Mum nearly died."

My heart squeezed. I wanted to hug him. I wanted to tell him it wasn't his fault.

"Your dad did a very bad thing. He did it. Not you." Ethan's voice was insistent but gentle.

"I let him into the house."

"Bailey, you were six years old. He tricked you. You didn't know what he was going to do."

"As soon as I opened the door, I knew I shouldn't have." Bailey was crying. "He was...he was really angry. His face was red and all screwed up." His voice was filled with tears and anguish.

What was Ethan doing? Was he comforting him? I turned to Rose. She was nearly finished. "Can you check the walking track for me, please? See if the signage is good? Don't go too far though."

She nodded and set off.

"It's OK, Bailey. It's OK," Ethan said, his voice soothing. "Your smart thinking saved your mom and Rose. You called the police. You saved them."

Bailey slowly regained control of his sobbing. Ethan led him out of the bathroom and sat on a log with him. I took that as my cue to join them and sat beside Ethan.

"Why did he have to come back?" Bailey asked.

"I think people like your dad don't like losing," Ethan said.

"What do you mean?"

"My dad was mean to me all the time. I would try to do what he wanted but it was never good enough. Was your dad like that?"

Bailey nodded.

"He did that because he wanted to control you. And he still wants to. That's why he came back."

"How can we make him leave?"

"I don't know. I hope the police will help us like they helped you that night."

I loved how honest Ethan was. He didn't hide the truth but delivered it with empathy. How did he learn that with such shit parents? Maybe his grandparents and brother. He didn't speak about them much, perhaps because he missed them.

I turned to face them. "In the meantime, Ethan and I will protect you and Rose."

Bailey's serious brown gaze settled on me. "And Ethan will protect *you*, Mum." He turned his attention to Ethan, searching his face.

Ethan nodded.

"You're nothing like my dad," Bailey said.

Ethan squeezed Bailey's shoulder. Did he believe Bailey's words? I did. I hoped he did too. He deserved to be free from his fears.

"I'm going to check on Rose." Ethan stood, looking around us.

"Ask Rose to help you put up some signs around the widow maker," I said.

"The what?" Ethan tilted his head.

I pointed to a eucalyptus tree. "They're known to drop limbs. If you look up in the canopy, you can see dead branches. They weigh the other branches down and can fall in windy conditions. If you're standing or camping underneath, it could kill you."

Ethan craned his neck.

"The widow part," I explained, "is because in the old days, most forestry workers were male. They die. They leave a widow."

Ethan looked around at the other trees. "That makes sense."

"We put signs around the ones we think might be a problem, so people stay away."

Ethan nodded.

"The signs are in the back of the truck."

He left us sitting together. I shuffled closer to Bailey and held his hand. "I want you to know I don't blame you. I blame myself for not leaving earlier."

"You were brave," Bailey said.

"You were brave, too." I gave him a fierce hug.

"We're lucky to have Ethan now," Bailey said.

"We are." I stood. "Let's get back to work."

But did we truly have Ethan? In less than four months, he would be gone.

I never thought I'd trust or feel this way about another man after Max. Max had broken me in more than one way. I believed now that I was the person I was meant to be. And Ethan never tried to take that away from me.

I trusted him. And I wanted him.

CHAPTER FORTY

Ethan

JASMINE and I sat on the porch together after the children were in bed. All was quiet except for the leaves rustling in the sea breeze.

She reached over and took my hand. "Thank you for speaking to Bailey today."

"You're welcome."

"He trusts you."

I nodded. Was I trustworthy? Doing what was right and protecting someone didn't mean you were trustworthy. I had a good moral compass, but it could disappear in a second. What if something set me off and I became my father?

"I trust you."

I stared out at the beach. Did she trust me because she needed to?

"Ethan, look at me."

I faced her.

"You need to stop living in the shadow of your father. You're not him."

"I don't want to hurt you or the children." I didn't want to be a monster.

She caressed my face, her thumb rubbing my cheek bone. "You are nothing like the thing you fear. You need to let go of that fear."

I searched her eyes, her face for any doubt. There was none. She believed in me. I needed to believe in myself too.

"I've been scared all my life, Jasmine. My marriage didn't work because of it."

"Do you feel different now? With me? Us?"

The way she saw me and understood me made me feel different.

"You make me feel safe. Your trust scares the shit out of me. But it also makes me feel strong."

She placed her hand on my heart. "You've been strong for thirty-five years. Now it's time to be a different type of strong. Be brave enough to let your feelings out."

I could do that for Jasmine. And I could do that for me. I'd told her so much more than I'd ever told anyone. She wouldn't shun or belittle me. She was gentle with my feelings. I took hold of both her hands.

"I can do that. You'll just have to remind me when I fall back into old habits."

"I'll help you."

I believed her. She already had. I was a different person than I had been two and a half months ago.

"You can help with something else too." I reached out and tucked a loose strand of hair behind her ear.

"What's that?"

I pulled her onto my lap and kissed her. Her lips were eager. I ran my hand up her bare leg. My heart beat fast.

This was the most I'd ever touched her. My fingers trailed under the hem of her shorts. Higher. Closer. Jasmine's breathing hitched; her lips paused. I'd gone too far. I withdrew my hand, ready to say sorry.

She pulled her lips away. Fuck. I should have stuck to kissing.

"Sleep with me tonight," she said.

My eyes widened. I tried to control my breathing. Did she mean sleep with her or *sleep* with her? Did I need to get condoms?

She must have taken my lack of words as consent because she grabbed my hand and led me inside. I locked the door behind us and followed her to her bedroom. She turned her back to me and took her shorts and top off, replacing them with a tank top and sleep shorts. She turned to me and gave me a small shaky smile before hopping into bed.

Shit. We didn't have to do this. Not if she didn't want to. I would have been happy with kissing her delectable lips. I took my shorts and t-shirt off, leaving my underwear on, and hopped in beside her. I lay on my back and reached for her hand. Should I say something? What?

I tilted my face to hers. "Just to be clear...are we sleeping in the same bed together, or are we *sleeping* together?"

Fuck, that sounded stupid.

"Do you want to?" she asked, her voice quiet. She didn't look at me.

"There will never be a time in the next million years when I don't want to have sex with you."

Still, she would not look me in the eye. She only stared into the space between us, the still air there replaced with her shaky breathing.

"I can't. I'm sorry," she whispered. "I wanted to. I mean I want to but—" She closed her eyes. "I'm sorry."

What had that monster done to her that she thought she had to ask forgiveness for being in charge of her own body? I hated him at that moment more than I hated my father.

I rolled onto my side and propped myself up. "Jasmine, look at me."

She did, although her eye contact wavered.

"Would you tell Rose to be sorry about saying no?"

She shook her head.

"Then you shouldn't be sorry either."

She nodded, but doubt flooded her face.

I smiled. "I'm not sorry. The hottest woman in the world has asked me to share her bed. I'm going to bask in it."

I kissed her gently on the lips and lay back down.

"And I get to share a bed with Sex on Legs." I could hear the smile in her voice.

She rolled over and put her arm around me. I pulled her in close. When she was ready, we were going to have the best damn sex ever.

Over and over again.

CHAPTER FORTY-ONE

Jasmine

I LAID the Christmas hats on the kitchen table—red with fluffy fur trim. The Christmas Eve bonfire was one of my favourite traditions. It was usually just the townspeople who came along, and we sat around giving gifts and singing Christmas carols.

"Are you ready for a small-town Christmas celebration?" I asked Ethan.

He studied me. "What does it entail exactly?"

"Oh, you know, a little bit of this and a little bit of that," I teased.

"Mmm." His lips turned up. "Another small-town adventure for me."

Rose came into the living area wearing a red Christmas dress with faux fur trimmings. She'd worn it for two years in a row and it was getting tight, but I couldn't convince her to wear something different.

"Do you know a lot of Christmas carols?" she asked Ethan.

"I know a few."

"Good. We can sing one together."

Poor Ethan. He didn't get much choice where Rose was concerned. First the Christmas tree and now singing with her. She grabbed a hat off the table and handed it to him before handing the rest out.

"Let's go," she said, grabbing his hand and dragging him to the door.

"It's OK. I'll take the bag of presents," I called after them. Rose didn't slow down.

"I'll help you, Mum," Bailey said.

He grabbed the Santa sack and flung it over his shoulder.

Jack had strung some Christmas lights out on poles around a long table and benches. He'd brought the tree down from the shop, and Christmas music played softly from a speaker. Bailey unloaded the gifts onto the sand. Everyone was chatty and cheerful as they handed food and drinks around. There was no need to sit close to the fire. The summer air warmed us enough.

"Different from a San Francisco Christmas?" I asked Ethan as we sat.

He nodded. "It's not cold, for starters."

We chatted away with everyone. Rose sat next to Jay talking about the dogs he'd looked after in the last week for people visiting the National Park. Sara and Lily brought down a cold ham and some salads. The love and laughter surrounding us warmed my heart. This was home. This was perfect.

When we finished eating, Rose stood up and declared, "Ethan and I are going to sing the Little Drummer Boy."

Ethan and Rose stood next to the tree and sang. Lucky Rose knew the words, which meant Ethan only had to sing the *pa rum pum pum pum.* My heart nearly burst watching them smile at each other and sing together. When they finished, everyone gave them a huge round of applause.

Ethan returned to the seat beside me, and we held hands while listening to the others sing as darkness fell.

"OK. Gift time," Jack called out. "Bailey and Rose, you can be Santa's little helpers."

They handed the gifts out one by one and then sat down so we could all open them. When the kids grabbed Ethan's presents, they perked up, their faces glowing as they shook the boxes near their ears and ripped the paper. Rose squealed in delight when she found a pair of mermaid summer pyjamas. I was surprised she didn't put them on straight away. Then, when she saw she had a huge thesaurus as well, she grinned. She ran to Ethan and gave him a hug. When she sat back down, she opened it up and searched for a word.

"This is an unparalleled gift," she said.

Ethan's smile was unparalleled. It stretched across his face as his eyes sparkled.

Bailey opened his next, his eyes glued to what was inside. It looked like a magazine of some sort, and he flipped through the pages. He looked up at Ethan and said a quiet "thank you". Then his eyes went straight back to the magazine.

"What did you get?" I asked.

He held up the magazine and a certificate. "A National Geographic subscription." His voice was in awe. He would be lost to us for the rest of the evening.

I sighed as I lay a hand over my heart. The gifts Ethan had chosen for each of the children showed exactly how well he knew them, the depth of their connection.

Ethan unwrapped his gift from me. It was a small

carving of the injured sea lion we'd called Angelo, complete with his fin tag and old injury. I held my breath as I waited for his reaction.

He turned it over in his hands and then gave me a kiss. "I love it."

"Now you can always remember us," Rose said.

"I'll never forget," Ethan replied.

I unwrapped a small box and looked inside. It was a large snow globe. Inside was the perfect scene of Haven Bay. The kids were there with Timmy on a board and Ethan and I were sitting together watching them. When I shook it, gold glitter floated around. Tears formed in my eyes. Ethan was the king of thoughtful gifts.

I let the tears fall as I leant over to kiss him gently. "Thank you."

"You're welcome."

My joy was interrupted by car lights lighting up the night as a car turned into the car park near the jetty. The door opened, and the figure of a man stepped out. Even though I couldn't see much detail, I recognized him immediately: Max.

CHAPTER FORTY-TWO

Ethan

My heart beat hard in my chest as Jasmine and I strode over to the car park. Silence replaced the cheerfulness behind us. If I knew one thing about people like Max, it was that they didn't like being the bad guy in front of an audience. That could be a saving grace.

"Max, what are you doing here?" Jasmine asked without any niceties.

"I'm here to see my children."

His voice, normally smooth, was edged with agitation. I stood closer to Jasmine, trying to block his view of the beach. His glassy eyes settled on me. "They're my children and I want to fucking see them."

Adrenalin raced through my body. I stood firm, trying to show I was calm and unaffected by him. "Max, you know that can't happen. Not until the court says so."

"Fucking court, what would they know?" he spat. He moved to the side so he could see the crowd on the beach.

The tic in his jaw, normally subtle, now seemed to jerk through his whole body.

I needed to calm the situation down. I knew how to do this. My child self was an expert. But not with someone who had taken a substance. He had to have been on something, some drug of some kind. I needed to keep his attention on me, try to train his erratic eyes to focus. Lower his agitation somehow. Keep Jasmine safe.

"Max, I know you want to see Bailey and Rose. I don't think now is the right time." I kept my voice calm and low.

"Don't tell me what I can and can't do with my fucking kids." His voice was loud. "You have no idea what I've been through. How some people fucking look at me." He turned his attention to Jasmine. "You fucking did this to me. You. You took everything I had away."

Jasmine took a small step forward. "Max—"

"Don't fucking Max me." He pointed at her chest. She took a step back. "I'll fucking take everything you have." He sneered at me. "And your fucking pretty boy won't be able to stop me."

My breaths were shallow. His previous visits had been nothing like this. "Max," I said, drawing his attention back to me. "I don't want to call the police, but you're not leaving me much choice."

He stood so close to me I could see the lines around his eyes and the spittle in the corner of his lips. "You call the fucking police and it will be the last thing you do."

In the state he was in, I didn't doubt his words. Normally, it was Jasmine he spoke to, not me. He seemed to have lost that inhibition.

"Leave now and I won't have to."

Someone was walking along the sand behind us. I glanced over my shoulder. It was Jack. Max saw him too and as soon as he did, he retrained his face. It was a thin disguise. His eyes were still bouncing from side to side.

"I'll be back." He made his way back to the car. "We could have done this the easy way. Now…" His voice was cut off as he got into his car and drove away.

The three of us stood and watched as the taillights disappeared.

"What now?" Jack asked.

"I doubt he'll be back tonight. Too many witnesses for his liking." That was the only thing that saved us. I stared at the retreating car with clenched fists. This needed to stop. "Jasmine, you'll need to talk to the police and get a new restraining order."

She nodded. "I'll do it tomorrow. Let's not ruin tonight for the kids."

We headed back down and tried to act normal. But none of us were the same. We were all lost to Max in some way. But my maze drew me deeper, past Max and down the years to my father.

HIS CAR PULLED *up into the driveway and then the car door banged. It was a sure sign that he hadn't had a good day.*

Steve was on his bed reading a book with his headphones on.

I rushed over to him. "You need to go. Dad's home and in one of his moods."

Steve pulled his headphones off, the music still playing. I switched it off. I hadn't done that once and copped it twice as bad when my father figured out that I'd been lying about Steve not being there.

"Come with me," Steve said.

189

"I can't," I said, listening to the footsteps on the stairs outside. "I didn't put my bike away. He'll know I'm home."

Steve's hands were shaking. I shoved mine in my pockets so he couldn't see my fear. There was no point going with him. You could never tell what mood my father was in. He could either calm down while we were gone or stew until we came back. This way, only one of us would have to face his wrath. And it wasn't going to be my twelve-year-old brother. If Steve was gone long enough, my father would forget he was angry with him in the first place.

"Go out the window. Go to Noah's place. Don't come back until I come and get you."

I left him and went into the kitchen to make a snack. Dad came in the front door and slammed it behind him, shaking the frames on the wall. The ones with photos where we pretended to be a happy family. There weren't many. He spotted me straight away. He always spotted me straight away. I squeezed my legs together to stop them from shaking.

"Eating again, are you? I swear I work a shitty job just so you can shove food in your mouth."

I didn't make eye contact with him. Making eye contact could set him off. Not making eye contact could set him off. You couldn't win, just had to figure it out moment by moment.

"Where's your brother?"

"He's at Noah's."

My father stormed into the bedroom we shared. I hoped Steve put his book on his nightstand. I finished making my peanut butter and jelly sandwich and sat down at the table. I wasn't hungry. Just the thought of eating it made me feel sick. But it might distract my father.

He came to the table and sat opposite me. "If you spent

as much time studying as you do eating, your brain might be bigger than your stomach."

I took a bite and chewed slowly. My straight A's apparently weren't good enough for him.

"I could have been anything other than a high school teacher if your stupid mother hadn't gotten pregnant with you. But I had to go to community college and work instead to take care of your sorry ass."

I'd heard it all before. And I knew it was best not to engage. My thoughts were a different story though. I mean, if he was so smart, why did he get my mother pregnant in the first place? And if he hated his job so much, why didn't he do something about it?

I took another bite. He leant back in his chair. Just like every other time he'd done that, I hoped it would give out beneath him and he'd knock his head on the way down. Maybe go into a coma or something.

No such luck.

He sat up and then came around the table to stand behind me. I tensed my shoulders. I didn't know what was coming and somehow that was worse. I took another bite, chewed quickly and swallowed, forcing the food down. All the while he looked over me, his breaths harsh. Sweat started pooling under my arms. I didn't dare move. All I could do was take another bite. Every time I swallowed it was like I was trying to swallow a baseball. He stood there until I finished my sandwich and walked away.

IT HAD all been a power game to my father. Max was the same. And it was the not knowing that was the worst.

CHAPTER FORTY-THREE

Jasmine

THE SUN WAS STREAMING through the window. I was lying in Ethan's arms. For two weeks we'd slept like this. For two weeks he hadn't pushed me to do anything more than kiss. He never asked why, never asked if I was ready now, didn't try to coerce me. I'm sure he wanted sex. His body told me so every time we kissed, but he never forced himself on me.

This was new. Everything in this relationship felt new. I could rely on him. I knew I didn't have to face Max alone, that Ethan would be by my side. And it wasn't through obligation. Maybe at the beginning it had been, but I didn't feel that obligation anymore. He wanted to be here with us. And every day our time together shortened.

Ethan stirred. He looked peaceful in sleep. Perfect. Who was I kidding? He looked perfect all the time. I sounded like a lovesick fool. Love. I did love him. I loved him for all he allowed me to be. And I loved him for all that he wanted to be.

Ethan's eyes opened and he looked at the clock. 6.30am. Still time before the kids got up. He pulled me in close and kissed the top of my head.

That wasn't enough for me today. Today I wanted to love Ethan with my body. I kissed along his jawline and then found his lips. My whole body leapt into life. I rolled on top of him, wanting to feel him everywhere. The kiss deepened and I nudged my tongue into his mouth. His low moan urged me on. His large hands cupped my arse and pulled me closer. His erection pushed against me. I rolled off so I could touch it.

I pulled down the top of his underwear and wrapped my hand around his thick shaft, ready to stroke. I paused. It was bigger than I expected. I'd felt it many times over the past few nights, pressed against me, but the clothes between us had belied its actual size. I started stroking.

He tore his lips away from mine. "Fuck," he groaned.

I wished we could. But it was too risky this time of morning. Even this was pushing our luck.

I held his dick firmly and pumped. "Later," I whispered.

"What?" he half moaned.

Just the sound of his voice, how he had lost a measure of control, made my stomach squeeze and my underwear wet. I listened for the children. There was no movement. But it didn't mean it would stay that way. I wanted sex. I was ready for sex...right now. But we couldn't.

Ethan moaned again, and a shiver shot through me.

"Later." I licked the skin under his ear as I pushed my breasts against him. "You can fuck me later."

His breathing hitched. I sucked on his neck and licked the salt from my lips. My hand didn't slow. He clutched at the sheets as his hips stiffened.

"Fuck," he grunted out as he exploded in my hand. His

hips bucked. His dick jerked as he emptied himself out. I didn't stop until he lowered his hips and relaxed beneath me. There was cum all over my hand and his stomach. He lay beside me, breathing harshly.

I wiped my hand on the sheet. "Lucky it's sheet washing day."

He looked at me and gave me a slow grin. "It'll be sheet day again tomorrow if we get to do what you suggested."

I could hardly wait.

"GOT YOUR BAGS PACKED?" I asked Rose as she came into the living area.

She clapped her hands. "Yep. Lily made us matching sleep shirts."

"Did she just?"

"Wanna see?" She brought her iPad over. Four shirts were on display. Each had their names—Jack, Lily, Bailey and Rose, a sleeping koala and the slogan *Sleep Over Crew*.

"Cute."

"Do you think she'll let us wear them to the bonfire?"

"Ask her."

Rose tapped away on her iPad. She cheered and ran off to see Bailey. I assumed she had gotten the response she wanted. She was back in a flash with Bailey in tow. I wasn't sure how keen he'd be wearing the shirt to the bonfire. But he wouldn't protest if Jack wore his.

"Can we go now?" Rose asked.

I shook my head. "Ethan is getting changed."

"Can't we just walk to the shop by ourselves?"

I couldn't let them. Who knew where Max was. He must be due for a visit again. It had been two weeks.

Maybe he was here already. Bailey sat on the couch doing a good job of pretending not to be bothered. He knew the answer.

"Ethan won't be long," I said. "Is your bed made, Rose? You know Timmy doesn't like to sleep on a messy bed."

"Yes. And I made Bailey's too. Boys are so messy."

Bailey rolled his eyes. "My side of the room is cleaner than yours."

"That's because my side is Timmy's side too."

"Because Timmy has so much stuff." His sarcasm was undeniable.

"He makes it messy." Rose pouted.

"Mum just said he doesn't like mess, so why would he make it messy?"

"He just does."

Nine-year-old logic didn't make sense. This argument could escalate at any moment. Rose and Bailey glared at each other, locked in silent battle.

"Are we ready, team?" Ethan asked, oblivious to what he had just walked into. When he didn't get an answer, he glanced between them. He must have summed up what was happening in a millisecond. Without engaging, he headed for the door.

"I'm ready," I said, following him.

One. Two. Bailey was behind me.

"Wait," Rose called out. "I forgot to give Timmy a kiss."

Ethan laughed and waited for her beside the door. As soon as she came out, she grabbed her chair and headed off with Bailey.

"Don't worry, we'll take your bags," I called after them.

Ethan and I walked hand in hand down the road. It wasn't pretend this time. We weren't putting on a show. And I liked it. We set our chairs up and sat down. I scanned the area. Was this what it was always going to be like? Would I always be looking for Max in the shadows?

"I'm going to grab a beer. Do you want one?" Ethan asked.

"Yes, please." As he walked over to Ross and Jay, my gaze strayed to his butt, appreciating how his shorts moved over it. My hands could be doing that later. I bit my lip.

Lily cleared her throat as she sat beside me. "So you don't hide your perving anymore?"

I blushed. "I don't know what you're talking about."

She gave me a knowing smile. "That's not the only thing that's changed, is it?"

"No." So much had changed in a few short weeks. "I—" Where was I going to start? "I didn't think I would feel this way about someone." I glanced at Ethan. He was watching me. My stomach lifted. Then he smiled and my whole being was captured in it.

"And what do you feel exactly?" Lily said.

I shrugged, bringing my attention back to her. The answer was too hard to put into words. "Content. Supported. Respected." I hesitated, unsure how to continue, but Lily waited patiently. "At first it was all about pretending, to protect the children. We faked our relationship." She already knew this, so why was I telling her again? Probably so I could work through it all with her.

"And now?"

"I'm not pretending."

"I'm not sure you ever were."

I considered her. I couldn't confirm or deny what she said. All I knew was what I felt now. Ironic, really, that I had Max to thank for this. Ethan and I may have gotten here eventually, but he forced us into it sooner. At least I could have more time with him as a partner before he left.

Ethan approached, his smile only for me, as if we had all the time in the world.

Lily patted my hand and got up to leave. "Make the most of your time together."

I would indeed. Starting tonight.

CHAPTER FORTY-FOUR

Ethan

THE LAST OF the light left the sky. Soft music was playing, and voices and laughter surrounded us. Jasmine held my hand as we talked quietly together. This was not what I'd ever expected before I came to Australia. It's certainly not what I'd expected when I met Jasmine. I hadn't even known how I was going to survive living with her and her *wild* children.

But the trust they had in me made me trust myself. It would be a battle every day to unlearn thirty-five years of hiding. But it was a battle I was willing to fight. And a battle I would win.

"Are you ready to head home?" I asked.

Jasmine nodded with a small smile. She stood and I packed the chairs.

"Rose, Bailey, we're heading home now," she said.

Rose ran over and gave us each a big hug. Bailey gave us enough attention to say goodbye. He was too engrossed in a story Ross was telling. Jasmine and I walked back hand in hand. Silent. The people behind us fading away, replaced with the lapping of the water. I focused on that and not my rapid heartbeat.

Jasmine locked the door behind us, and we headed to her room. She turned on her lamp before turning off the light. The soft glow illuminated her.

We stood there looking at each other, not moving. I felt like a teenager who had no idea what to do. But I did know. I'd thought about it more than once. I approached her and placed my hand on the small of her back. Her warm brown eyes looked into mine. My fingers tangled in her hair as I tilted her head up to kiss her. She closed her eyes and sighed into my mouth.

That's all the invitation I needed. I yanked her into me. Her soft breasts pressed against my chest. I kissed her hard, with desperation and yearning. Her response was identical. My dick hardened.

Fuck. If kissing felt like heaven what would touching her feel like? What about being inside her?

I forced our mouths apart. She stared up at me, her full lips wet, her cheeks flushed.

I reached out to undo the buttons down the front of her dress. Her chest heaved. I undid the top three buttons, revealing the top of her breasts. Another two buttons and her dress fell from her shoulders. I ran my fingers along the bra line, causing a small shiver from Jasmine. Another two buttons and her dress fell to the floor.

I sucked in a breath. I'd seen this much before but not like this. This was intimate. Beauty, strength and bravery stood before me. She may have been shy, a little scared even, but she stood before me, letting my eyes take in every inch of her. Her black bra and underwear with a touch of lace were perfectly Jasmine—sexy but not flaunting it.

I skimmed the top of her underwear with my fingers and got a small tremble in response. I needed to see all of her. I needed to watch her body respond to me. I reached behind her and unclasped her bra. The straps fell from her shoulders, and I cast it to the ground.

I lowered my mouth to her right breast and sucked on it. Her nipple hardened in my mouth. Her moan travelled all the way to my dick. It was at full attention now. I moved my lips to her stomach, kissing her down to her belly button. Her breathing hitched.

As my fingers hinged at the top of her underwear, I was rewarded with another small tremble. I'd need to remember that spot. I slipped her underwear down until she could step out of them. Then I dragged my hand up her inner leg, my fingers taking their time on her soft silken flesh. They reached the spot between her legs. Warm. Wet. I groaned. My dick needed to be inside. My tongue wanted to taste it.

I slid a finger along the wet folds and pushed it in. Jasmine grabbed hold of my shoulders. I repeated the action. Her fingers tightened and a small moan escaped.

I moved her to the bed. Two fingers this time. She moaned louder. My dick throbbed harder. She responded to my every touch like I was wielding some kind of magic— pressing against me with a moan or shiver.

I pushed her down onto the bed and manoeuvred her higher then lowered myself to my knees. My fingers went back to giving her pleasure. She had been timid days ago, scared, but not now, now there was trust and desire. Lightness spread through me knowing I'd helped her get here.

She opened her legs wider, baring herself to me. I slid my tongue up from her entrance to her clit. She tasted divine. Fuck restraint. I licked and sucked, taking in every last drop she would give me.

Her hips rose and she cried out my name. She was so close. But still holding back. I circled her entrance with my tongue. A drawn-out moan. Louder. Every moan settled in my stomach, expanding, reaching my groin. Fuck, I wanted her like I'd never wanted someone in my life.

I returned to her clit. Jasmine grabbed hold of my hair. Her legs trembled. She held tight, and I worked her a little bit more. I wanted to make her tip over the edge. She screamed out my name. Her whole body shook, the vibrations urged me on. I kept going until she let go of my hair and lay wasted before me.

My breath was coming hard and fast. *I'd* just done that. *She'd* just done that. I stood up and looked down at myself. I was still clothed. My dick couldn't care less as it throbbed in my shorts. I wiped my mouth with the back of my hand. Jasmine's eyes were half closed as she looked up at me.

Time to awaken her again. I went to the bedside drawers and got a condom.

CHAPTER FORTY-FIVE

Jasmine

NEVER. Nothing. What? I'd never experienced anything like that. That... what he did, what he made my body do. Everything inside me had surged, like erratic eddies moving in every direction.

Ethan gave me a small smile as he undressed himself. My eyes were drawn to his fingers rolling the condom on. My heart rate sped up. I'd never been so excited about having sex in my whole life. If what just happened was anything to go by, this wouldn't only be about him getting his rocks off. Was I being selfish? I shouldn't be thinking just about myself.

Ethan approached the bed never taking his eyes off me. My stomach squeezed. I shuffled up the bed. He kneeled on it and kissed my stomach, my chest, my neck. Then he reached my lips, and I could feel the smile on his as he kissed me lightly.

"Lucky the kids aren't home. Your screams would have woken them up."

A soft laugh escaped my lips. I'd lost control and it was amazing. "That was a new experience for me."

"Mmm."

He captured my lips and kissed me hard and deep. Every part of me responded. I yearned for him.

Ethan pulled his lips away and raised himself onto his elbows. "OK?"

I nodded.

He guided himself in. I grabbed onto his shoulders as I stretched around him and he moved inside me. I'd done that earlier when I'd lost control. I blushed. I wanted to let go of him, to have some sense of composure, but his rhythm and size had me hanging on tight.

He slowed down. I searched his face as he let out a little huff. He slowed further.

"What's wrong?" I asked.

He shook his head. "Need to slow down a bit. I don't want you to think I'm a one-trick pony."

I ran my thumb over his lips and then followed with a kiss where I tugged at his bottom lip. "I don't care how many tricks you have if they all feel as good as this."

He pumped inside me. "As good as this?"

I sighed. "Yes."

His rhythm picked up again. In. Out. In. Out. Hitting some magical spot each time. My fingers dug into his back. I met him thrust for thrust. He lowered his head, and his ragged breathing caressed my neck.

"Fuck... you...feel... so good," he grunted.

He groaned stroke after stroke. Each thrust moved me higher up the bed until he anchored me there. With every movement, his groin rubbed against my clit. Holy shit. Heat spread through my body. I cried out. Spasm after spasm around his dick.

"Fuck," Ethan groaned. He slammed into me, his whole body shaking.

"Fuck," he whispered as he lay on top of me, our sweat and hot skin slick.

"Not a one-trick pony," I whispered in his ear.

He let out a chuckle. Then kissed me. Our breathing didn't have a chance to normalise. Nothing about Ethan and me was normal. And that scared me. My feelings especially.

———

I WOKE up like I had most mornings wrapped in Ethan's arms. Sex hadn't changed that part of our lives, but what about all the other parts? Would there be expectations now? I didn't just mean about sex. Although, the fact that he hadn't wanted me to reciprocate straight after my first orgasm surprised me. In the past it had been more like OK you've had your turn, bad luck if you didn't orgasm, my turn now. I don't even think the thought crossed Ethan's mind.

Did sex bring other expectations? Like some sort of commitment? That sounded very old-fashioned. Was there now supposed to be some confession of love? My feelings were so confused.

I'd let Ethan lead the way. Was that wise? He wasn't known for sharing his feelings. That might actually be best in this situation. I nodded. Good plan.

I rolled onto my back and stretched. The morning sun was halfway across the room. I glanced at the clock. 8am. I couldn't remember the last time I'd slept so late.

Ethan shifted and opened his eyes. He gave me a lopsided smile. "Morning."

Flashes of our orgasms flew through my mind. It certainly was a good morning.

Ethan rolled over and kissed me. His hand skimmed up my leg, over my hips and under my top. His big hand wrapped around my waist, pulling me closer. His thumb rubbed the underside of my breast. Seconds later, his whole hand was cupping it. He rolled my nipple between his thumb and forefinger. It hardened instantly. The way my body responded to him was unreal.

Ethan yanked my top off and his mouth took over from his hand. When his mouth crossed over to the other one, the air caressed my wet nipple. My skin prickled.

Ethan drew his hand down my stomach and into my underwear. "So wet for me already."

He slid two fingers in and scissored them back and forth. Holy shit. I reached down and shoved my underwear off. His hand had freedom of movement. As his fingers pumped, he rested his thumb at the base of my clit. Holy shit. My small moans filled the otherwise silent room.

"Do you like that?"

"Yes."

"What about this?"

His fingers moved inside of me. He hit *the* spot. I nodded. And moaned out something that sounded like yes. I couldn't breathe. Couldn't think.

I pushed my back into the mattress and opened my legs wider. His thumb moved in the same rhythm as his fingers.

"And this?"

I nodded. That spot. His thumb. Holy shit. I clutched at the sheets. As I opened wider, my whole body was gasping for air. My stomach tightened. I clenched my teeth. Why? I didn't know. I couldn't breathe.

He moved his fingers again. I clamped around them. And spasmed. A silent cry escaped my mouth. My whole body trembled. Is this what an earthquake felt like?

I opened my eyes as Ethan rolled onto his back. My breathing was ragged. I concentrated on each of my limbs, feeling them one by one, restoring my body to normal.

I reached for Ethan's hand. Sex on legs.

I giggled.

Ethan swung his head to mine and raised his eyebrows.

CHAPTER FORTY-SIX

Ethan

Jasmine's giggle turned into a barely controlled laugh. "I'm sorry," she said between gasps. "You're really living up to your name."

I stared at her. What was she talking about?

"Sex on Legs."

I rolled my eyes. I hadn't come up with a name for her yet. I smiled when it hit me. "Well, the OQ would know."

"The what?"

"Orgasm Queen."

Jasmine rolled over and planted a kiss on my lips. "Sex on Legs created her."

I smiled. I'd never had that effect on anyone before.

She rolled onto her back and stretched. "I'm going to shower." She gave me a smile. "I should probably pick up the kids."

Always a mom. One of the things I respected most about her. And one of the things I liked most. Another thing was that body of hers.

I imagined her naked with the water flowing over her curves and my tongue trailing the stream. I imagined fucking her senseless against the cool tiles. And—

No. I adjusted my hard-on. Enough. I had work to do. I was falling behind on my data collection and report.

"I'll make us breakfast. Then I might head to the office to do some work on my project."

"OK."

Was that disappointment in her voice? She rolled out of bed. I expected her to walk away, but instead she knelt on the bed and gave me a warm, lingering kiss. Then she got up and smiled. "Tonight we'll need to use our quiet voices."

I laughed as she walked out of the room. Tonight. Tomorrow night. And every other night... for three more months until I had to return to my old life.

We never spoke about it. I'd never promised more than this. But was my silence a promise? Was it telling her there was more when there wasn't? Or did we not speak about it because there was no point? We both knew how this would end.

I went to my bathroom and took a quick shower before heading into the kitchen to start breakfast, Jasmine's favourite—bacon and eggs on toast. All of it tasted different in Australia. The bread wasn't full of sugar, the bacon was salty and fleshy, and the eggs were fresh. It was like a food paradise.

I looked out the window to the beach. Paradise out there and paradise in here as well. Maybe I was seeing things from a different perspective and forgetting the other important things. I just needed to refocus, that's all. I wouldn't forget I was here for my dissertation.

I STUDIED the stats in front of me I'd been collecting over the past few months and switched over to my report. It needed to be ground-breaking. Information that hadn't been shared before. What I had was good. But I needed to make it great.

I began writing, but the silence soon distracted me. That didn't even make sense. I came to the office for peace. I found a radio station on my computer and turned the volume to low for background noise.

I was only fifty pages into the report which should extend to three hundred. What did I have so far? We'd recorded the biological stats of the sea lions when we'd tagged them. We saw the movements of those we'd placed transmitters on, and I'd been out to visit the places they frequented most. I'd noted the changes in sea lion behaviour on tour days and non-tour days.

Next, I needed to visit the colony two inlets over to see if the sea lion behaviour there was the same when people invaded their space like we did most days here.

That meant more research. But I needed to formulate a plan on what information I would record. It was all about the behaviour of the animals and whether human visitors changed that behaviour. I needed a drone first. The drone would allow me to record normal behaviour before we arrived, behaviour on boat approach and behaviour on arrival. Jack could help me with his drone. Then I should do that for the Haven Bay colony too and compare the results.

Children's laughter filtered through the open door, drawing me to the window. Bailey and Rose were creating a huge sandcastle on the beach. Timmy lay on a blanket in the middle of it, watching their antics, like he was king of the castle. I chuckled. That kitten was as good as any dog. Jasmine sat next to them, reading a book. Is that what they'd been like before Max and I turned up? Relaxed and carefree?

Maybe not before I'd turned up seeing that Jasmine had been working seven days a week. But was it much better after I'd arrived? Not really. She was out there helping me a lot. Moments like the one I was witnessing were rare. A partner was supposed to make life easier, and I wasn't sure I did. I was her partner at work, but the load wasn't evenly split, even if I took in the part-time factor.

I needed to let them have more time like this, on their own, free. I could ask Jack for help with the drone, and I could do more of the research on my own. It might serve two purposes—time together for them and increased concentration for me.

CHAPTER FORTY-SEVEN

Jasmine

BAILEY STOPPED on his way back from the water with a full bucket. He was watching something near the jetty. "Where are Ethan and Jack going?"

Ethan and Jack were on the jetty, heading to the boat.

"I don't know. Why don't you go see?"

Bailey put the bucket down and ran to them. They spoke together and Ethan shook his head, looking towards us. Bailey's shoulders dropped and he trudged back to us. Ethan and Jack unmoored the boat and headed out of the bay.

Bailey picked up the bucket and went back to the castle. Rose studied him. She bit her lip and glanced at me.

"What are Ethan and Jack doing?" I asked.

Bailey shrugged and worked on the castle, not looking at me. "They're going to the inlet with Jack's drone."

I knew from the hurt in his voice that he'd asked to go, and Ethan had said no. Why would he do that? He'd always included Bailey before.

"Maybe they just thought it was better for adults this time."

Bailey shrugged again.

Rose stood up and wiped her hands on her shorts. "Let's fill the moat."

I jumped up and grabbed a bucket. "We'll have to be quick or else it will all disappear."

Bailey poured his in and we all ran into the water. I scanned the bay; the boat was on its way out.

I WAS CHOPPING vegetables for dinner while the kids relaxed in front of the TV. I'd seen the boat enter the bay a short while ago; Ethan would be home soon.

How was I going to approach what had happened this afternoon with him? He had no obligations to the children. Just because we were living together and having sex didn't mean that he had to take the children on as his own. And because he'd included Bailey before didn't mean he had to keep including him.

But his leaving Bailey out had hurt him, and I needed to address that. It may not have been a deliberate thing. I doubted it was. But it would be a sensitive subject especially since he was always fighting to not be like his father and this might trigger Ethan. I didn't want to hurt him. This was the first time I'd had to address something like this with him. I'd need to go lightly, which was not my strong suit.

But Bailey had to know as well that sometimes Ethan needed time on his own. What he was working towards was important, not just for the sea lions but for his future as well.

I finished chopping the vegetables and put a pot of hot water on. Ethan's footsteps sounded on the stairs, and his key was in the lock. Rose turned and gave him a smile as he entered. Bailey kept his attention on the TV.

"How was the sandcastle making?" Ethan asked.

Rose twisted in her seat. "Fantastic. It was huge and we made a moat and filled it with water. Timmy was the over-lord. He didn't do any work, just lounged around."

Ethan chuckled. He glanced at Bailey, who was still ignoring him.

Ethan took his bag to his room and joined me at the kitchen counter. "Need some help?"

"Can you dice an onion for the Bolognese, please?"

"Sure."

Now was the time. I didn't want to make an issue out of it. I just wanted to understand his reasoning.

I took a deep breath. "Bailey was disappointed not to go out on the boat with you today."

Ethan looked between me and Bailey. "You were all having such a good time. I didn't want to interrupt it."

See, logical explanation. I didn't know why I was so worried.

"You're always so busy." His gaze was steady, holding me. "You don't get much alone time with the kids."

My heart filled. That time he'd given us wasn't just a small token of love, it was a big one filled with considera-tion. I gave him a side hug, my arms lingering around him. "Thank you."

Ethan hadn't started chopping. He was watching Bailey instead. "Was he upset?"

"I think he felt hurt to be left out."

Ethan didn't give me or the onion any further considera-tion. He went to his bedroom. I didn't want him to disengage. We needed to tackle things like this by being open. That's the only way we could succeed in this relationship.

I glanced at his room. Maybe I should follow him, talk about it more. But if I did, would he shut down?

CHAPTER FORTY-EIGHT

Ethan

My DAD LEFT me behind all the time, whether he was going out with his friends or even chatting with students. I was nothing, insignificant. Never in my life would I want someone to feel like that. Especially someone I cared about. I'd thought I was doing the right thing, and by Jasmine's response, I had. But it was still wrong in the eyes of an eleven-year-old. He was on the cusp of going from a child to a teenager. Life was confusing enough for him without me making it harder.

I grabbed my laptop out of my bag and headed into the living room. I stood beside the couch. "Do you want to see some of the footage we got today?"

Rose clapped. "Yes."

Bailey shrugged.

"Sorry, you couldn't come out with us today. I thought you should have some mom time."

Bailey glanced at Jasmine who gave him a smile. His

attention turned to the laptop in my hand. He'd normally be jumping out of his skin to look. Now he was completely blasé.

I'd really fucked up.

I plugged the laptop into the TV and went to the drone footage. "We started with the little inlet. Jack positioned the drone above the sea lions so we could see their reaction to our approach. What do you think happened?"

Rose moved forward in her seat. "They all got excited and hopped in the water to meet you."

Bailey rolled his eyes. "They are wild animals, Rose, not pets."

Smart kid.

"The sea lions here do that," Rose protested.

"No, they don't." Bailey shook his head. His full attention was on us now. "They sit and watch us. Some come into the water but most of them don't."

Rose crossed her arms. I smiled. She was always the dreamy one, seeing love and positivity.

"Watch," I said.

We saw the moment they heard the boat approaching. Many of them lifted their heads from their prone positions. Then when the boat came into sight, many of them sat up and kept a watchful eye.

"We get closer to shore, but we do it very slowly."

"Why?" Rose asked.

"We didn't want to scare them. Imagine if they all rushed into the water at once."

"They could get hurt," Bailey said.

"Exactly. They can't tell the difference between a boat and a predator. They need to protect themselves. The water is where they feel safe."

The boat stopped twenty metres from shore. Some sea lions fled into the water. The young who were close to those sea lions followed.

"Why do you think the young ones did that?"

"They copied the adults," Bailey said.

Rose nodded. "Like if your mum was scared in a storm you would probably be scared too."

I smiled at her. "Precisely."

"Precisely," she repeated.

Was that going to be her word of the week?

Bailey was still watching.

"So, next, I need to visit them at different times of day to see if their reaction changes. Then I want to visit every day to see if that makes a difference."

"To see if they get used to you," Bailey said.

"Yes. And I want to record our colony to compare."

Jasmine came over and sat on the arm of the chair. "What will all this tell you?"

"It will help determine the best distance for boats so as to not disturb colonies."

"And that will mean less injuries and less disturbance during breeding season," Jasmine said.

I nodded. "Yes."

"And that may help stop sea lion numbers declining."

I nodded.

She rubbed my back. "And this will form part of your dissertation."

"Part of it."

She kept her hand on my shoulder.

I looked at Bailey and Rose. "If Mum says it's OK, you can help me over the holidays."

Bailey turned to Jasmine, hope filling his eyes.

"I don't see a problem with that," she said. "But sometimes it will be just Ethan and me, and sometimes Ethan on his own."

Rose clapped.

"Thank you," Bailey said to me.

"You're welcome."

That kid was something else. This family was something else. The only other time I'd felt this content was with my grandparents. It had taken a while to trust them. They had been patient with me and let me take my time. Most of all, they'd never let me down.

Like Jasmine today, they weren't angry if I'd done something wrong. They didn't put me down. There was no power struggle.

I glanced at the three of them. If I'd ever wanted a family, I'd want this one.

"ETHAN."

Fogginess. Where was the sound coming from? I forced my eyes open.

"Ethan," Bailey said, coming to my side of the bed. His eyes were wide. He kept looking over his shoulder.

I manoeuvred myself from under Jasmine and sat up. "What's wrong?"

"I heard a sound outside."

Jasmine rose into a sitting position.

I swung my legs out of bed and looked at the clock—2am. "What sort of sound?"

"I don't know. Footsteps. Tapping."

Jasmine hopped out of bed.

I grabbed my board shorts and tank top off the floor. "OK. I'll go check."

"You're going out there now?" Jasmine stood beside Bailey.

"Well, yeah." Didn't we want to know what was out there? "It's probably some sort of animal."

"Maybe we should leave the animal alone. It will be gone by the morning." The slight tremor of her voice showed her fear.

I looked between her and Bailey. I needed to reassure him somehow. "I'll go turn the outside lights on. The nocturnal animals won't like that." And while I was doing it, I'd check the doors and windows. Just to be sure. "Wait here."

I turned the lights on and stared into the pool of brightness. There was no movement. But who knew what was beyond in the darkness.

Creaking behind me. Tingles raced through my body. I swung around. Jasmine took a step back.

"I told you to wait with Bailey."

She peeked over my shoulder, looking into the shadows.

"I can't see anything out there," I said.

"He wouldn't make it up." Her voice was full of accusation.

"I didn't say he made it up. I said I can't see anything."

She turned on her heel. "I'm going to sleep with the kids."

I watched her retreating back.

I tried to tell myself we were all on edge. We were all waiting for something, but we didn't know what. And that was why she was upset with me. I lay on the couch and closed my eyes. I went over everything in my head from the moment Bailey had woken us up, trying to figure out what I'd done wrong.

Were my actions like what I'd expect from my father? My brain failed to make a connection.

CHAPTER FORTY-NINE

Jasmine

I HOPPED into bed beside Bailey. Being close to them was my best option. I needed to know they were safe.

I couldn't believe Ethan playing hero, wanting to go out there to see what the noise was. Opening the door to let a maniac in was not going to happen. Did he really think he could protect us from that?

The gentle sea breeze was amplified as darkness enveloped me. The leaves rustled. I shivered. Every sound could be Max.

This was ridiculous. We hadn't seen Max in weeks. That meant one of two things. He'd given up. Unlikely. Or his anger was brewing. More likely. But it didn't mean the sounds Bailey heard were him. Ethan telling me to stay put had got my back up. And the way he said nothing was out there was as dismissive as Max had always been. OK. Maybe not. Ethan wasn't Max.

Bailey's breathing evened out. The lights Ethan had

turned on crept in around the blinds, so we weren't in complete darkness. My eyelids drooped.

Where was Ethan now? I drifted in and out of sleep.

I awoke to soft talking. "Jasmine, wake up."

I peeled my eyes open. Ethan was standing beside the bed. Sunlight streamed through the gaps in the curtains.

"Come into the hallway," he said almost in a whisper.

I followed him.

"Max's car is out front. I've called the police." He paused, as if waiting for me to catch up. "I can see him in the car, just staring at the house."

I went to make for the hallway. Ethan took hold of my arm. "He doesn't know that I've seen him. I don't want to tip him off."

We were sitting ducks.

"How long ago did you call the police?"

He showed me his watch. The stopwatch said seven minutes. They'd be at least another twenty-five. Would Max wait that long before making his move?

Bailey and Rose were both sitting up in bed, listening. Rose clutched her trauma bear.

"The way I see it, we have two choices," Ethan said. "We wait here and hope the police arrive before Max blows." He grimaced. "Or you take the kids out the back door and head into the bush. I'll give you a few minutes to get free. Then I'll go out into the kitchen and pretend it's like any other day, giving you more time. He won't find you before the police arrive."

Bailey got out of bed and got dressed. Rose didn't move.

"Rose, honey, Bailey is going to help you get dressed."

"Put on your sneakers or hiking boots," Ethan added.

Had he already chosen for us?

He pulled me down the hallway. "You will be able to

get away before he knows you are gone. Once he's out of the car, it's too late."

"Why can't we all escape?"

Ethan pointed to the living area. "If one of us doesn't go out there soon he'll get suspicious. This may not be the first time he's watched us. He might know our normal movements, what time we wake and get going."

He was right. We needed to keep Max distracted. Out there in the bush, we'd have a chance. But we'd be sacrificing Ethan to Max and his erratic behaviour. My hands shook. I clutched them together. Rose and Bailey stood in their doorway.

"I need to get dressed." I strode to my room and got dressed quickly, my sweaty, shaky hands making an ordinary task difficult.

A car door closed. Fuck, we were too late. I gulped in air. Ethan was next to me before I'd even called his name. Rose and Bailey were right behind him.

"We need to get the kids to safety," I said.

"Go," Ethan said.

"It's too late."

I needed to stay now. I needed to distract Max, so the kids had time to escape. If I went with them, he might figure out more quickly that we were gone and hunt us down. If I pretended they were still here, they could get away.

I'd planned for this. Planned it until there was nothing left to plan. Their escape was what was important here. I grabbed Ethan's wrist. Seventeen minutes to go. In seventeen minutes, Max could have the children. He could take them by boat seeing that car wasn't an option—one road in, one road out. In seventeen minutes, we could all be dead.

I took hold of Bailey's shoulders. "Bailey, you need to

take Rose. Go to Jack and Lily's. Take the long way so no one can see you."

"No, Mummy. I want to stay with you," Rose begged.

I crouched down in front of her. "I can't protect you."

"But Ethan can." She latched onto him. He smoothed her hair and picked her up. Outside, Max was yelling incoherently. Rose clutched onto Ethan. He pushed her back gently.

"I need to keep your mom safe. The only way I can do that is if you and Bailey are not here."

Tears ran down her face.

We were running out of time.

"Go out the back. Run into the bush," I said.

Bailey nodded. "Make our way to the shop."

"Like all those games we played," Rose said, wiping her nose with the back of her hand.

"Exactly like that."

Ethan put her down.

She hugged him. "I love you, Ethan."

He hugged her back. "I love you too."

Didn't he understand the urgency? He looked at me over the top of her head. He knew. And then it registered— he was going slow for them, being as calm as possible for them. But also playing with time. Time for the cops to arrive.

He cupped the back of Bailey's head. "You can do this. No matter what you hear, do not look back. Do not *come* back. Got it?"

Bailey swallowed. He nodded and took Rose's hand. I hugged them both with all the strength I had.

"When I open the front blinds, sneak out the back," I said.

I wiped my sweaty palms on my shorts and walked out into the living room. Ethan led the children to the laundry. With all of Max's yelling, he wouldn't have heard the back door unlock. I snuck one last look at them and then pulled on the cord.

Max's attention came to me in an instant. The back door opened and closed. Ethan locked it. Max didn't approach the house. Good. More time for the children. More time before he realised they weren't here.

"Give me my fucking children," Max bellowed. "Rose! Bailey!"

Max was so tense he looked bigger than his size. His t-shirt was wrinkled and hanging askew. His attention was on me, but his eyes were unfocused. I wasn't sure if he was taking drugs the last time I saw him, but I didn't doubt it at all now.

In essence, only panes of glass and a door separated us. It was nothing. Even if the children's sandcastle were real, all of its defences would be nothing. I looked around for Ethan.

"If he sees me he might lose it," Ethan said from the other end of the living area. I nodded. He always knew the right things to do and say.

"I want my fucking family, you stupid lying slut." His eyes were usually cunning, thinking of his next step, but now they were almost bulging from his face. His face twisted as he bared his teeth. I gasped as he stormed towards the house.

"Two minutes," Ethan said.

Two minutes had passed since the kids escaped. The kids would be safe in the bush now, heading to Lily and Jack's.

"You fucking whore. I want my children."

Do I just stand here? Do I say something? Would anything calm him down?

All my plans shrivelled to nothing as I watched a demented Max. He threw the furniture on the deck aside and smashed his fist against the window. The glass rattled.

"Jasmine, come here," Ethan said.

I moved backwards. Max caught sight of Ethan.

"You fucking homewrecker. You stole my family." Max stormed towards the door and then disappeared. But his voice rose high and angry. "Rose! Bailey!"

"Shit." Ethan's voice was full of urgency. "Jasmine, get out of—"

Max crashed into the door. The door shook. Ethan strode towards me. Another almighty bang and the door crashed down. Like a feral animal, Max jumped to his feet and honed in on his target—me.

CHAPTER FIFTY

Ethan

I RAN TO JASMINE. She froze as an unhinged Max rampaged toward her. He threw a punch. His fist connected with her jaw. A thud louder than my rushing pulse resounded. Jasmine's head snapped to the side. She wobbled on her feet. I was still a few feet from them. My legs needed to go faster, but I felt like I was going in slow motion. Or Max was going at the speed of a killer whale.

Max grabbed her throat. He punched her again. Blood sprang from her cut lip. "I'm going to fucking kill you."

Jasmine's eyes were unfocused. Her hands snatched at his. She kicked out at him. He didn't even flinch as her foot connected.

"Max," I yelled. "Let go of her."

It was like he didn't hear me.

I rushed at them. Max didn't notice me. There was only one thing on my mind, saving Jasmine.

"You fucking bitch." Spittle flew from his mouth. "You can't keep my children."

I collided with him. His hands flailed, releasing Jasmine's throat. She crumpled to her knees, gasping for air. Max and I slammed into the floor. He thrashed beneath me like a shark caught in a net. I couldn't contain his throes. Knees and elbows connected with me.

Fuck. Where were the police?

Jasmine. I searched for her. She was rising to her feet, unsteady.

A punch connected with the side of my head. I pushed out of Max's grasp. I threw my elbow at his chin. His head swung sideways. I elbowed him again. And again.

A growl roared out of his throat. His narrowed eyes focused on me. I needed to get to my feet. Get outside. Away from Jasmine. Keep Max away from her.

I shoved on his shoulders. The distance between us increased. I shuffled backwards like a crab. Max's eyes were on me, where I wanted them to be. He followed. Stealthy. The hunt was on.

"You can't take my fucking children from me," he roared.

I stood up and backed out of the house. He tracked my every move.

"They're mine." He charged at me.

We plummeted off the porch and smashed into the ground. Pain erupted through me. Max's weight forced the air from my lungs.

Sirens in the distance.

He sat up and slammed punch after punch into me. My ears were ringing. His face was blurry. I bucked beneath him.

"Max, stop," Jasmine screamed.

He was distracted. I blocked a punch with my arm and grabbed his fist. He was off balance. I threw him off and rolled to my hands and knees. Blood dribbled from my mouth. My head was foggy. I didn't get to my feet quickly enough. His foot connected with my ribs. Cracks reverberated through my body.

"I'm going to fucking kill you both," Max ranted. "You can't stop me then."

His rants mixed with the sirens. Loud. Lights flashed dimly in my vision.

"Stand back," a police officer yelled.

I fell to my side. Max calmly stepped back and put his hands up. The crazed animal was gone. He looked me straight in the eyes. "I'll fucking get you." Then he turned to the police, knelt down, and folded his hands behind his head.

Jasmine ran to me. Max looked between us and gave us a haunting smile. "She doesn't love you," he said. "You're nothing now that you've done your job."

I tried to take a deep breath to calm my racing heart. Piercing pain shot through my chest. I gasped. I wanted to get up, to show him that the pain he'd inflicted meant nothing because we'd won. The children were safe. Jasmine was safe. But I couldn't move.

The last time I'd felt agony like this it was caused by my father.

Would the memory of Max plague me as long as my father's had?

CHAPTER FIFTY-ONE

Jasmine

ETHAN WAS SITTING on the porch, staring out at the water. He'd been quiet and distant since he'd come home from hospital. He'd spent two days in there due to his broken ribs and torn spleen. Thankfully, he hadn't required surgery. I'd tried to talk to him to figure out what he was thinking or feeling. But the old Ethan was back. He kept everything inside.

Rose went outside and sat on the chair next to him. She took hold of his hand, saying nothing and staring out at the water with him. A soft smile lifted his lips. She'd stuck close to him since he'd returned. She didn't talk his ear off, just watched him closely or sat with him.

When he saw Bailey for the first time, he'd told him what good a job he'd done and how proud he was of him. Bailey had glowed.

Apart from that, we hardly spoke as a family. I guess we were processing it all in a different way. And processing led to regrets. For me anyway. And I needed to share them.

Max may have been sent back to jail, but did that mean we were truly free? What about the next time he got out? What about the memories that would haunt us? I was grateful the kids weren't there to see him hit me or Ethan. That was a trauma they didn't need to live with.

But the fact that they'd had to leave their place of safety was bad enough. Our home had always been a safe place until Max had shown up. Would his being sent back to jail be enough for them to feel secure again?

I touched my throat. Max's big hands had nearly snuffed out my life. I kept thinking that I should have escaped with the kids. And with Ethan too. Coulda. Shoulda. Woulda. It's a game none of us should play.

Rose came inside, and I went out, sitting in the chair she'd vacated. A week ago, I would have taken Ethan's hand. Now I wasn't sure if he'd accept mine.

"Are you OK, Ethan?"

"Yes. I'm fine."

"Do you need some painkillers?" That's not what I really wanted to ask.

"No, thanks, I don't think I need them anymore."

"OK. Do you want to go out on the boat? We can get Jack to take some more drone footage."

"Maybe tomorrow."

"OK."

This was so much harder than I'd thought. I needed to thank him for saving us, for sacrificing himself. And I needed to apologise because I hadn't done the same for him.

If I didn't start saying the words, he may stay shut off forever. And I didn't want that. I wanted our last months together to be filled with love and laughter and kindness and respect. I wanted to enjoy him and his presence. I wanted to remember everything he'd given me, including trust.

Most of all, I wanted to tell him I loved him. But I wasn't sure this was the right time.

"Thank you for protecting us."

"No problem. That's what I'm here for."

My stomach knotted. Did he really think that?

I faced him. "I never meant to put you in that position. I didn't want you to get hurt."

He stood and walked to the door. "I know."

My words weren't connecting. He was fighting some demon I couldn't see.

My heart followed him, but the words stuck in my throat. Would I ever be able to say them?

CHAPTER FIFTY-TWO

Ethan

I WALKED ALONG THE BEACH. My ribs still ached but that was it. My other bruises and swelling had disappeared. What hadn't disappeared were Max's last words.

Jasmine wasn't like my mother. She'd shown me that over and over again. The way she treated her children was nothing like I'd experienced. She'd protect them with her last dying breath. Whereas it had been my job as a child to protect myself and my brother. And the one day I did more than just play my father's games was the one day I realised I could be just like him.

IT WAS JUST MY FATHER, *Steve and me sitting at the table. My mother was sick in bed. She hardly got up these days. Her chance of treatment was gone the day he stole the money that had been donated to her. Steve had cooked us dinner, but he'd made a mistake with the recipe.*

"What the fuck is this shit?" my father yelled as he threw

his plate. It hit Steve's jaw and fell to the floor breaking into pieces. "You can't even cook a simple fucking meal."

He stood up and stormed toward Steve. Fear took hold of my heart. His tempers had become worse and worse over the past few months. I never knew what he was capable of anymore.

I shoved my chair back. It crashed onto the floor. Steve was holding his jaw. Blood was seeping through his fingers. I couldn't get around the table fast enough.

"Don't touch him," I screamed.

My father paused for a moment. I'd never spoken out like that before. That pause was all I needed. It gave me time to take the last few steps to get between him and Steve. I stood eye to eye with my father. Size was the only thing on my side.

He punched me hard to the side of the head. I wobbled. I watched, stunned, as my father pulled Steve out of his chair. Steve's eyes were round and full of tears. He was smaller than me. If my father punched him with the same ferocity as he had me, he could really do some damage.

I shook my head to clear it and pushed Steve away. Then I hit my father in the head, over and over again. I couldn't stop. White hot rage filled my veins and powered my fists. I yelled at him as I hit him. I don't even know what words I said. But they were pure hate. Sixteen years of pure hate escaped.

Blood spurted from my father's nose and his eyes were swelling shut in front of me.

"Ethan, stop," my mother said. Her soft voice stopped me mid-punch. "If you'd cooked instead of Steve, then your father wouldn't be angry."

As soon as the words left her lips, she collapsed. Steve went to her and tried to rouse her. But she was gone.

My father's laugh was mirthless. "You idiots have killed your mother."

Steve bowed his head as I stood in the middle of the room, my fists covered in my father's blood.

STEVE. I went to the office, logged into my computer and called him. His face came on the screen almost immediately. I shifted in my seat and winced.

He studied me. "Man, you look like shit. Did one of those sea lions attack you?"

I shook my head. "Jasmine's ex came back."

"Shit." He moved closer to his screen like somehow that got him closer to me. A mere inch when we were thousands of miles apart was minuscule. "Are you OK? What about the others?"

"I'll live. Cracked ribs are the worst of it."

"And the others?"

"All OK. The kids got out to safety before he got into the house."

"And Jasmine?" he persisted.

I sighed. "She's OK. Thankful. Relieved. He won't be getting out of jail anytime soon."

The assault meant his parole had been revoked and he'd gone straight back to prison. Add these new charges and he'd be there for years.

"I wish Dad had gone to jail," he said. "We might have lived in peace."

I'd thought that once too. "Probably not. Mom would have brought another man into our lives, and it would have been the same."

He nodded. "Gran and Gramps said that too."

If only we had gone to live with them earlier.

"But Jasmine's not like that," Steve said.

That's true. She didn't need a man in her life to feel fulfilled. She didn't need me. Now that Max was gone, she definitely didn't need me.

"No, Jasmine is nothing like Mom."

Steve watched me in the silence. "That's a good thing, right?"

"Of course it is. Bailey and Rose feel loved and protected."

"But what about you?"

"What about me?"

"Do you feel loved and protected?"

I shrugged. "What does it matter? I'll be leaving in two months."

Steve frowned. "Stop hiding behind the time."

"I'm not."

"Ethan." His voice was firm. "We never lie to each other."

I sighed. "I don't know. I don't know how serious she is."

"How does she make you feel?"

Now or before? And why was it different now? Because of what a psychopath said? Or because of my deep-seated fears?

"I felt seen and understood."

"Do you still feel the same?"

No lying, right? "No."

"Why?"

"I've never felt loved like that before. I don't trust it."

"I love you."

"You're my brother."

"It doesn't mean I need to love you."

I laughed. I'm sure at some point in our lives he didn't love me.

He gave me the dad look he was a master at. "You need to talk to Jasmine. Tell her how you feel."

I nodded.

"Maybe record it for posterity. You know, the day Mr Buried Feelings actually lets them out."

"Ha ha. Funny."

He waved me away. "Off you go."

I walked back to the house. Jasmine was on the porch watching the kids and Timmy on the beach.

I sat beside her and took a deep breath. No point hiding anymore. "When I was younger my dad would go on rampages. Not all the time. Usually, he just resorted to mental abuse." I reached for Jasmine's hand. She gave it to me without hesitation.

Trust.

"Mom didn't protect us like you protect Rose and Bailey. She always thought he'd changed. Every single time I could see it coming, and she didn't."

Rose and Bailey laughed at Timmy. The freedom in the sound warmed me. I held Jasmine's hand tighter.

"I'd hide with Steve. Sometimes there wasn't enough time for us both to hide, so I'd let him get away."

I shivered. It would be twice as bad for me when that happened.

"Mom would always tell me it was my fault, and that I made it worse by trying to hide."

I don't know why you'd say that to a child instead of trying to protect them. I could try to turn things over in my mind. I'd done it a thousand times. But my mother's actions never made sense.

"At first, I argued with her, tried to make her see reason. It made no difference. Then I stopped. I stopped sharing my thoughts and feelings. The only person I spoke to was Steve.

I co-existed with everyone else on the basis that I had no choice."

I still did. I knew now that I was the major contributor to the failure of my marriage. Audrey hadn't had much to work with.

"My grandparents didn't force me to share, so I didn't. And I didn't want to, until you."

Now for the ultimate truth. It came pouring out. Every last moment of that fateful day. "I hit my father over and over again. Just like he'd done to Steve and me a hundred different times. And I didn't want to stop. I was just like him."

I'd just shared all of that but what was the point? They were just facts, a part of my history. I was supposed to share how I felt now. I sighed. What was the point? Honesty was the point. Love was the point. But I didn't trust love. Not when the people who were supposed to love you didn't.

I didn't know what to say or where to start. So, I didn't. I just sat there staring at nothing.

Jasmine squeezed my hand to get my attention. "Thank you for trusting me enough to share." She paused, letting the words sink in. Trust. It was all about trust. "I'm sorry for not protecting you like you protected us."

I hadn't said all that for her to feel guilty. No wait, I needed to use my voice. Say the words out loud. "I didn't tell you all of that to make you feel guilty."

"I feel guilty every day for not stopping Max sooner. I didn't want you to get hurt. I'd never want that. I love you too much. I don't want you to ever feel that I wouldn't sacrifice myself for you."

I tried to grasp all of her words. But got stuck on one.

"I'm not sure I know what love is."

She cupped my cheek. "Ethan, love is what we have.

Two people who are scared but willing to try. Trusting each other not to give up. Sharing ourselves piece by piece."

I nodded. "Love is us."

She leaned over and captured my lips with hers. She kissed me gently. Her lips held promises I'd never even dreamt of. Touching parts of me I never knew existed.

CHAPTER FIFTY-THREE

Jasmine

I DREW my lips away and made eye contact with Ethan. His vulnerability was clear on his face. Pain and fear were part of his life. I'd do what I could to erase it. I caressed his cheek. "I know we don't have forever. But I don't want to waste what we do have."

"Me either," he said.

I needed to love Ethan as much as I could for the next two months. And because I never said I wasn't selfish, I needed to soak up as much of his love as I could to get me through the rest of my life. I wanted him to stay, but I wasn't going to stand in the way of his dreams.

"Ethan," Rose yelled. "Come and watch Timmy."

And I guess I'd have to share him.

We walked down the stairs hand in hand. Poor Timmy hadn't come out all day after Max had been taken away. When the kids had arrived home, he'd gone to each of them to make sure they were OK, then never strayed far from them. When Ethan had come home, Timmy had sat with him for hours on end.

Bailey and Rose were waist-deep in the water, holding the board Timmy was standing on. They walked alongside him as they moved the board through the water. He balanced himself perfectly over the little waves. When they turned the board around and gave it a push, he surfed all the way in. When it hit the sand, the little ball of orange wearing a makeshift life jacket jumped into the water and ran to us.

Rose clapped. "That's the furthest he's gone by himself."

Ethan bent down to pick him up and winced. Regardless of the pain, he grabbed Timmy and lifted him, giving him ear rubs. Timmy nuzzled into him. Ethan breathed deeply and winced again. Damn. The doctor said it would take six weeks for his ribs to heal. By then his stay would be coming to an end. We would be coming to an end. My chest tightened.

ETHAN and I were standing in the kitchen, making bacon and eggs for breakfast.

"I don't know why you get the queen bed. I'm the one who needs to share a bed with Timmy," Rose said from Bailey's room. He'd moved back in there a week ago, and this was a constant argument. The house next door was finally finished but it didn't matter. Ethan wouldn't be moving there.

"Like he takes up so much space."

The toast popped up and I buttered it.

"He does. He likes to stretch out." She glared at Bailey.

"He shares the bed with me too and we don't have any issues."

"Because you have a queen bed," Rose said. Her tone implied that Bailey was an idiot.

Ethan served out the bacon and eggs. "We could just move the other queen bed in from next door for Rose."

"You indulge her too much." I failed at hiding my smile.

It was a good idea, though. Especially if it meant we didn't need to hear about fairness and equality and favouritism for another four weeks, or ever.

"I'll call Jack after breakfast to see if he can help," I said.

"I'm sure we can manage."

It had been six weeks, but moving furniture still seemed excessive for someone recovering from fractured ribs.

"Why don't we see how you feel after our swim today?"

He nodded. Swimming with sea lions could be intense with sudden and jerky movements if they wanted to play. He might not feel up to it after that.

"Breakfast," I yelled out as I set the plates on the table.

Rose sat down at the table first. "I—"

"I don't want to hear it," I said, holding up my hand.

She sank back into her chair and pouted.

"Ethan suggested we bring over the other queen bed from next door for you," I said.

She sat up straight and looked at Ethan. "Can we, Ethan?"

Not can we Mum. Oh no, I didn't count anymore.

Bailey rolled his eyes. "Now who's the favourite?"

"Shut up. You were the favourite first."

Ethan looked between them with tight lips. He'd mastered the stern dad look, alright. "If you're not careful, both of you will have single beds."

Bailey screwed his face up at his sister. She poked her tongue out. Ethan held in his laughter. I would miss this simple family time together. I'd miss Ethan more than I was willing to think about. We finished the meal in peace and then headed out to the boat. Ethan had tried swimming with the sea lions two weeks ago, but it had been too much for him. He was sure today was the day.

We anchored in our usual spot. Most of the older sea lions paid us no attention, but a few juveniles perked their heads up. Rose and Bailey jumped in and turned back to the boat.

"Come on, Ethan," Rose said.

Bailey looked at him with expectation.

He tore off his shirt, sat on the stairs, and pushed off from the boat. No sea lions had come in yet. Ethan swam after Rose and caught her leg. She squealed. It was Bailey's turn next. He was faster than Rose, who cheered Ethan on. I hopped in the water and swam in the other direction. They had too much energy for this time of the morning.

Ethan left them and swam over to me. He took me by the waist and pulled me towards him, a tentative smile lifting his lips. "Jasmine Taylor, I love you with every fibre of my being." He kissed me while we tread water. His tongue exploring like he was probing the depths of me. The parts of me no one else ever saw, the parts no one was interested in seeing.

Water whooshed past us. We broke apart. A sea lion was circling us. I looked closer at the scarred fin. It was Angelo. He nudged Ethan, swam away and came back again.

Ethan laughed. "Finally, the seal of approval."

Angelo nudged him again and Ethan swam after him in a game of chasey. I'd always prided myself on not needing a man, but I needed Ethan. Every part of me needed him. But I wouldn't tell him that. We'd always known our time was limited. It wouldn't be fair to put that pressure on him.

CHAPTER FIFTY-FOUR

Ethan

I SETTLED into bed with Jasmine. Six months had gone by so fast. I wanted another six and six more after that for the remainder of my days. But my career and what I'd been striving for were not here. My heart felt like it was tearing.

Jasmine took my hand. "I'm going to miss you."

My chest constricted. We'd never really spoken about being apart. The pain in my chest was the obvious reason why.

"I'm going to miss all of you and this place." It was true. This was the first place that had ever felt like home. *They* felt like home.

"We can still talk over video." Her voice was soft, uncertain.

"Every day if you want to."

"I'm sure the kids will."

"We can do other things by video too." I gave her a soft nudge.

She rolled towards me and laughed. "Sex on Screen doesn't work as well as Sex on Legs."

"It just doesn't sound the same. Should we practice now?" I gave her a quick kiss.

"Not the screen part." She straddled me and leant down, her breasts brushing my chest. I reached out to turn the lamp on. I needed to burn this image into my brain. I knew every curve by touch. I needed to know them by sight as well. And smell. I reached my hand into her long brown hair and tangled my fingers in the softness. Pulling her closer, I took a deep breath in—ocean air and a hint of citrus.

Jasmine's mouth crashed into mine. Her mouth was as relentless as the sea. She opened her legs wider and rubbed against me. The inside of my mouth vibrated as she moaned into it.

Her lips left mine. "Condom," she almost begged.

"Top drawer."

She didn't wait for me. Within seconds, she had it in hand, ripped the packet open and was rolling it on. Then she was taking me inside her, inch by inch. Fuck, she felt good. She rested her hands on my shoulders, balancing as she rose and fell. With eyes half closed she bit her lip, letting out a sinful moan.

My dick hardened. I didn't know it was possible to get any harder. I reached my hands up to cup her breasts, squeezing them as she quickened her pace. So soft. So malleable. I let go and watched them move rhythmically.

I ran my hands down her side and rested on her hips. My thumb found that spot of hers I'd promised to remember. I applied the smallest amount of pressure. Jasmine's mouth dropped open. Her moan bordered on indecent. My balls tightened. Her hair fell around her face like a curtain trapping us in our own world.

Her pace slowed just a fraction, and she lowered her face to mine. Her breaths were as fast as my heartbeat. The warm air against my ear sent tingles through me.

"Fuck, Jasmine." I thrust into her. I squeezed her hips and held her where I needed her.

"Ethan."

Her moans matched her breaths. She lifted herself up and we locked eyes. Her body tensed above me. Tremors followed. I exploded. Spasms rocked my body. No rising and falling. No thrusting. Just coming at the same time. All the while we watched each other.

Jasmine lay down on my sweaty chest. I held her close, my hands flat against her back. No one could ever fit as perfectly as she did.

THE BED SHIFTED BESIDE ME. I cracked an eye open. Rose was climbing up the bed to lie between us. The sky outside was showing the first signs of a new day. Rose settled down close to me.

Footsteps entered. Bailey. His footsteps were softer than his sister's. Jasmine moved over so he could lie next to her.

Rose turned to me. "I wish you were my dad."

I gave her a hug. "I wish you were my daughter." Said the man who never wanted children.

"If you stayed you could adopt me."

Oh shit. I thought they understood.

Jasmine opened her mouth.

But I beat her to it. "I can't stay. I have work to do back in San Francisco."

She nodded. "I know. You need to teach the world about sea lions. It's important."

"Yes, it is important."

Bailey shifted. "If I become a doctor too could we work together?"

I thought about how long that would take. I'd be close to retirement. But Indiana Jones wasn't good at retirement. I could follow in his footsteps.

I sat up slightly so I could see Bailey. "Absolutely."

"Maybe we could do some more research here so we can be a family again," he said in a hopeful voice.

"Sounds like a plan." A plan thwarted by a million impossibilities. But I wasn't going to ruin his dream. It was a good dream. A great one.

Timmy jumped on the bed and nestled between Rose's legs. "Timmy will miss you too."

"You'll need to send me some surfing videos so I can show him off."

I remembered the flash of orange on that first day as he'd run after the two wild children. I smiled.

"Will Angelo still be alive then?" Rose asked. "I bet he'll miss you."

Angelo always sought me out now when we went swimming. He'd grown in confidence. It was good in one way, but a problem in another. Humans' position here shouldn't encourage interaction.

Bailey shook his head. "Sea lions don't live as long as humans."

"How long?" Rose asked.

"Twelve to sixteen years."

"Oh."

The bedroom was alight with the golden light of sunrise. I took a deep breath. It was another thing I'd miss about this place. Was there anything I wouldn't miss? I could stay lying here forever with the people I loved most in the world, but time wouldn't stop for us. My destiny awaited. It sounded like I was going on a life-changing quest. But the truth was I'd already been on one.

Jasmine shuffled up into a sitting position. "How about you go make us some breakfast while Ethan and I have a quick shower?"

Bailey rolled out of bed and picked up Timmy on his way out the door. Rose gave me a quick hug and then followed her brother.

Jasmine went to the door and looked back at me. "Coming?"

CHAPTER FIFTY-FIVE

Jasmine

I WALKED into the shower and turned around, waiting for Ethan. His skin had tanned even more over summer, except for the part covered by his shorts. The pale skin there offered a stark contrast.

His dick was raised at half-mast, but I wasn't here for that. Even though I'd never say no. Who could say no to Sex on Legs? I'd never get sick of looking at his fine body. The broad shoulders were that of a strong man, but they didn't begin to describe the strength he held within.

Ethan stepped into the shower. We stood under the streaming water together. I wanted him alone for just a few minutes before he left.

I gazed up into his striking hazel eyes. They were the first thing I'd noticed the day I saw a picture of him. Unlike Lily, who'd seen everything else first. Ethan cupped both of my cheeks and brought his warm lips to mine. Tears pricked at my eyes. I didn't want him to leave. But I couldn't ask him to stay.

Ethan pulled his lips away. His thumbs wiped gently at my tears. My throat constricted. He ran his thumb over my lips and swallowed. He looked into my eyes.

"Love is us." His voice broke.

I GREETED the guests as they started arriving for the tour. You'd think head office would have had their shit sorted out and replaced Ethan before he left. It's not like they hadn't known the date. It had been two weeks already and I was still alone. Once the guests had all gathered around, I explained to them how to put their wetsuits on. My chest tightened. Ethan usually did this part while I got to enjoy the view. His legs and great arse, his back and chest, him catching me watching him.

Enough memories. I took a deep breath and pushed through.

Once the guests were ready, I got them settled onto the boat and headed to the swimming spot. I filled the silence by telling everyone about the sea lions, sharing facts I'd learnt from Ethan when he was here.

"We recently had a marine biologist stay with us for six months," I said as I brought the boat into position. "He was a wealth of information. He helped us tag the sea lions here. The colony has 380."

The guests looked out to the beach.

"OK. If you're ready, make your way down the steps and into the water. Move away from the boat so there is room for everyone behind you."

As the guests entered the water, the sea lions approached and started swimming with them. One was particularly frisky today. I smiled over at Ethan. Only Ethan wasn't here anymore. I sighed. There was no one to share these little joys with.

I thought it would get easier with time, but even after two weeks I missed him. I missed the little moments, like sharing a simple smile. I clenched my jaw. Six months wasn't enough. I could have had longer being close to him if my defences hadn't been so high. If I'd seen what Jack and Lily had seen between us from the start.

I wanted him back. I wanted to be with him every single day of my life. But I couldn't ask him to do that. I couldn't ask him to give up everything he'd worked for. I ran my hand over my face. Was love really this impossible?

I sounded the horn for the swimmers to come in, then stood on the stairs and helped them if they needed.

A middle-aged lady beamed up at me. "That was one of the best things I've done in my life."

I smiled. "It's amazing how close they get, isn't it?"

"Oh yes. I could see every bit of my sea lion's cute little face."

Ethan would have kept talking to the guests, but I just didn't have it in me. Not the energy or the inclination. I helped them all on and headed back. Once I'd packed everything away, I headed into the office. I turned on my computer and looked at the bookings. I'd need to send messages to tomorrow's guests to confirm.

Ethan's empty desk loomed large. My eyes were constantly drawn to it, and my chest constricted each time. I wished it would stop doing that. I'd be walking around with a strained chest, unable to breathe at this rate.

The office felt so vacant. How could one person fill the space so much? Even when Ethan had been working quietly on his report, I'd been aware of his presence. I turned my attention back to my computer. There was no point thinking about Ethan. He was there and I was here. Oceans apart.

CHAPTER FIFTY-SIX

Ethan

I SAT with Steve on his back porch while Sloane and Harley kicked around the soccer ball in their small suburban backyard.

"More people play soccer in Australia than other types of football, but more people watch Australian Rules and rugby," I remarked.

"That's strange."

"There are so many strange things." I laughed. "They shorten the names of everything. Like Bailey, they'd call him Bails."

Steve looked over at me. "You miss them, don't you?"

I nodded. "They filled up all the hollow spaces. Everything felt alive with them."

We spoke almost daily, but it was never enough. I missed the incidental conversations, the random things we'd talk about.

"Bailey keeps a list every day of things he wants to talk to me about or ask questions about."

"Geez. I'm lucky to get more than a grunt from Harley."

I laughed. I was lucky to even get a grunt.

"How's your dissertation going?"

"Almost finished. I'm combining my previous research with what I just did in Haven Bay, plus what I have found published in scientific and academic publications."

"Then what?"

"I submit it for review. Then I need to defend it in front of a doctoral committee."

"All this to become a professor. I thought you taught for a while, got experience, got old, got a PhD, and moved into the role."

"A PhD also opens up an array of research opportunities."

I'd wanted this forever. Since my childhood when my father had continually told me I'd amount to nothing. I decided I'd amount to more than him. A university professor, a doctor, over a high school teacher. But it didn't give me satisfaction anymore.

"Do you know why I wanted to become a professor?"

Steve shook his head. "I just thought you were the boring brother."

"Dad always told me I was a worthless piece of shit."

He shuddered. "I remember."

"Being a professor trumps being a high school teacher."

"So, your whole career was to spite our asshole father?"

"Yes and no. I chose marine biology because of Gramps and his sailing stories. I chose to take that to the next level to prove myself."

"Why bother? That man is not worth our energy."

"I know that now."

But all my life I'd been trying to be the opposite of him or proving him wrong. I could have been living a fulfilling life instead. And now I wanted to be, with Jasmine. But maybe setting a time limit on my relationship with Jasmine was what had made it so successful. I didn't need to think about the next five years or fifty years. She might have loved me for that reason. Because there was an end. Did I want something I couldn't have?

MY COMPUTER ALERTED me to an incoming call—Jasmine and the kids. I saved what I was doing and switched over to the call. Rose shoved Bailey aside and set herself up in the middle of the screen. He rolled his eyes. He was patient enough to wait his turn. But she obviously had something important to say.

Rose grinned at me. "We did art at school today. We had to make a picture of our family." She held a picture up for me to see—a beach scene with people.

"You're the mermaid," I said, pointing to the waving mermaid. "And there's Bailey and Timmy on the board."

She nodded emphatically. "And you and Mum holding hands, watching us."

I sucked a breath in. It was too much. The simple beauty of it. I nodded and smiled, even though it was forced. "I love it."

She clapped her hands. "I'm going to mail it to you. That way we can be close all the time."

Tears pricked my eyes. "I will put it on my fridge."

She was beaming. "When are you coming back?"

"I don't know." The kids wanted me there but did Jasmine? She never asked me.

"You work at a school, right?" Rose said. "Can't you come here on school holidays?"

I nodded. Not saying yes was less committal. I'd have to actually face my fear of not being wanted and speak to Jasmine.

"My turn now," Bailey said.

Rose moved a mere two inches to give her brother some space. I searched for Jasmine in the background. She was at the kitchen counter, probably making afternoon snacks. Her head was bowed, and she didn't look our way. I sighed inwardly. Perhaps Rose's request wasn't that exciting for her.

I turned my attention to Bailey. "How was school today?"

"Mrs Goode said that we are going to do a big assignment this term on animals. She said we could choose land, sea or sky."

"What are you going to choose?"

"Sea. She said I can't just do sea lions though; I need to do the ecosystem."

Hundreds of thoughts ran through my head. If I was there, I could help him. My chest squeezed. Absence does not make the heart grow fonder. Absence breaks the heart. I was torn in two, wanting to be with the family I loved, but not wanting to give up what I'd worked so hard for.

I listened to Bailey as he told me about the assignment. All the while I snuck looks at Jasmine. She came over to the table and set two plates down.

"It's late for Ethan. Let me talk to him so he can go to bed."

My heart lifted, and I shifted in my seat as I waited for her to take over the screen.

CHAPTER FIFTY-SEVEN

Jasmine

ANOTHER DAY without a call from Ethan. He sent us all a message saying he was busy with his dissertation. His mentor had edited and reviewed it, but there were some final touches to make before submission.

Once he finished, everything would be back to normal. *Normal* would be having him here with us. It had been five weeks since he'd left, and I knew we were drifting further and further apart. Two different oceans. Two different worlds.

I walked to the shop to collect the mail. I needed company. I needed to talk to another adult. Winter was coming, and I didn't have the distraction of tours anymore.

The cool wind, unusual for this time of year, encouraged me to pick up my pace. The bell jingled as I entered. Jack looked up from his crossword puzzle.

"Hi, Jack."

"How are you going, Jasmine?"

I shrugged.

He pursed his lips and put his pen down. "How's Ethan?"

I shrugged again.

"You know, you're going to have to use your words."

He led me to the living area. Lily was busy sewing some hanging pouches for native rescue animals. No wonder she hadn't come out. She wouldn't have heard the bell. She stopped the sewing machine when she saw us.

Jack motioned me to the couch. "Jasmine was about to tell me how Ethan is."

I sat on the edge. "He's busy. We haven't spoken for a few days."

"Poor Ethan. He must be working so hard." Lily left her sewing and sat beside me.

My stomach tightened. I'd been worrying about how much I missed him. Not about how exhausted he must be.

"I wish he was here."

Lily took my hand. "I understand why he couldn't stay."

I sighed. "Me too. That's why I didn't ask him to. He's been working towards this his whole life."

Jack sat on the arm of a chair. "Once he gets his doctorate are you going to ask him to come back?"

"I can't. That wouldn't be fair."

Lily gently rubbed my hand. "Are you scared he will choose his career over you?"

"Why wouldn't he? We both knew we'd be over after the six months."

"So, you're just going to pine for him?" Jack asked. The voice of reason.

"No." I took my hand from Lily.

"Maybe he doesn't know returning is an option. You need to communicate that."

Was it a choice he wanted to make though? I'd have him

back tomorrow if I could. But there were two people in this 'love is us' equation. I rested my head in my hands. The worst that could happen if I asked him was that he said no. At least I'd know then.

"I'll ask after his submission."

I collected the mail and walked back to the office via the beach. I could ask Ethan to come back. The question was, would he be happy here with us? I sat on the sand and stared out at the water. I'd given everything I could and hadn't feared rejection because it was inevitable he was going to leave. I hadn't asked him to stay because I didn't think we were enough for him. How could we compare to a prestigious career? In reality, I was hiding behind his job as much as he was.

The soft lapping of the ocean soothed me. The only solution in my mind had been for Ethan to come back here. Instead, we could always move to be with him. I gazed around the bay—quiet, secluded and calm, the water darker now that winter was upon us. This was our home, our haven. It didn't mean we couldn't make a home somewhere else. Ethan wasn't the only one who could make a sacrifice. We could too. We could give up our slice of paradise. Being with him was the most important thing. That's what I wanted most. And so did Bailey and Rose. Their hearts were full of love for him.

After his dissertation submission, we needed to talk. I needed to put my heart on the line.

CHAPTER FIFTY-EIGHT

Ethan

I sat on the sofa with a scotch and let my body relax and melt into the cushions. It was finally done. My dissertation had been submitted for review. I stared at the printed copy on my desk. Over half a ream of paper. I'd never worked so hard on a piece of writing in my life. Even when my father had stood over me telling me my work wasn't good enough.

After all that, it was time to wait. Wait for it to be reviewed. Wait to find out when my defence would be. Regardless of how long it took, I'd be prepared.

I glanced at the laptop on the sofa beside me. It had been weeks since I'd spoken to the kids properly. I always made an effort, though, to at least touch base. I never wanted them to feel they weren't important. I'd been scared of having a family. But the love Jasmine, Bailey and Rose gave me proved I was nothing like my father or my mother.

Exhausted as I was, I wanted to speak to them. It was Saturday there. They might not be home. I called anyway. It rang and rang. I held my breath. Finally, it connected.

Jasmine's face appeared on the screen. Her long brown hair fell around her shoulders. She wore a blue hoodie zipped up to her neck and her tan seemed to have faded. She gave me a smile. "Hi."

"Hi."

"Is that Ethan?" Bailey yelled from the distance.

Jasmine started walking. I could see she was heading to his room. "Let me speak to him for a few minutes first, OK?"

"Yes."

We were walking again. To our room, Jasmine's room.

"How's the dissertation going?"

"All finished. I just submitted it."

"Congratulations." She studied me closely. "You look exhausted."

"It's been a long two months. Working, writing and juggling it all."

She nodded. "Thank you for finding the time to call us as well."

"The best part of my day." It was time to lay it all on the line. "I don't like being apart from you, Bailey and Rose."

"I don't like it either." She bit her lip. Her picture shook. "I haven't spoken to the children yet, but what would you think about us moving there to be with you?"

I stared at the screen. I'd never even thought about them moving here. Jasmine giving up her peaceful life had never been an option in my mind.

"It was only a thought," she said, her voice tense.

My eyes darted to her. "Sorry, you took me by surprise."

She frowned. "It doesn't sound like it was a good surprise."

I moved myself to the edge of the chair and set the laptop on the table. "I don't think you moving here is a good idea." I tried to align my thoughts. They were coming too fast.

"Fine." Her voice was terse. Her shoulders were high and stiff. She was holding back tears. "I'll go get Bailey."

"Stop."

She stood and headed to the door.

"Jasmine, stop." My voice was firm. "Look at me."

She did. Her face contorted, then settled. "It's not like there's another choice. We move there or we don't. If we don't, then we're not together."

"I can move there."

She narrowed her eyes. "And give up your career? The one you've worked towards for the past ten years?"

"It's not as important to me anymore."

Her expression didn't change.

"Jasmine, I want to be with you and the children. That's what's important."

Her chest rose and fell. She shook her head. "You're tired, Ethan. You're not thinking straight. I don't think it's a good idea for you to move here, give up everything, and then resent us later."

I needed to make her understand.

She started walking again. "There is nothing here, Ethan. Just a beach, some sea lions and us. No big city, no university, no aquariums, no research centres. How can that ever be enough for someone as driven as you?"

She was being stubborn and unreasonable, just like when we first met. I would laugh if my whole future didn't rely on us talking this through.

"Jasmine, can we talk about this?"

She paused and glanced at the phone. "Call me when you're rested and have thought it through."

"I'll call you tomorrow."

She shook her head. "When you've thought it through."

She handed the phone to Bailey and walked away.

I SAT on my brother's back porch. He handed me a beer.

"Jasmine has a point. What will you do there?"

"Be a ranger. Research. Teach. Get out of this hectic life."

"You haven't really thought this through, have you? Where are you going to teach in the middle of nowhere?"

"The universities in Australia are progressive. A lot of courses are delivered online."

"And how do you even know they'd be interested?"

"Because I contacted them to ask."

Steve regarded me. "What, in your spare time?"

"I made time. Steve, this lifestyle won't be good for Bailey and Rose. They wouldn't have the same freedoms here."

"Wouldn't it be better for them to have opportunities rather than them being so isolated?"

"But at what price? It's safer there. The crime rate is low. Guns are highly restricted. Wages are higher. They have a better work/life balance. Everyone working full-time gets four weeks paid annual leave a year and two weeks sick leave."

"They're just kids. They won't be working for a while."

"But I need to think of their future."

"Spoken like a true dad."

I smiled. "That's exactly what I want to be."

Steve gave me a sidelong look and smiled. "Never thought I'd hear those words coming from you."

"I'm not scared of being like our father anymore."

"Good. Because you never were."

I took a deep breath in. I'd come to believe that in the last few months, Steve's affirmation cemented it. Talk about being freed.

"I still think you need more of a plan," he said.

"I have one. I just need to convince Jasmine."

CHAPTER FIFTY-NINE

Jasmine

It had been two days since we'd heard from Ethan. Two days since he'd rejected my proposal for us to move to San Francisco to be with him. I should have kept the conversation going while I had the chance. The silence was worse than him not being here. I had no idea what he was thinking. Or even if he was thinking of us.

I should have stopped to listen to him. But the rejection had cut deep. And I knew why. I didn't think I was enough for Ethan. Sure, I was enough while he was here but we both knew that was short term. Filling a space in someone's heart forever was a different story. And maybe he felt the same. That's why he didn't call.

I tried to be reasonable and calm my thoughts. But it was hard. The pragmatic side of me said if this is what ruined us, then we were never going to succeed. The emotional side rejected every sensible thought as my heart broke again and again.

I moored the boat and tied the lines before making my way down the jetty. Someone stood there waiting. Ethan.

I stopped dead in my tracks. I couldn't take my eyes off him as he stood there in a wide stance, hands in his pockets, watching me. Ethan. *Here.* He walked towards me—slow, determined, his eyes searching mine.

What the hell was I standing here for? I ran into his open arms and clung to him like he was a lifebuoy in the middle of a vast ocean. He held me tight and rested his head on mine. I squeezed him tighter. My throat clogged as tears wet my cheeks. He kissed the top of my head.

I withdrew and looked up into his face. His pink lips. His thick eyebrows. His smooth kissable skin was covered in short stubble. Tears spilled from his hazel eyes. He cupped my cheeks with both hands and wiped my tears with his thumbs. He brought his lips to mine. Salt from his tears, our tears, mixed. His kiss filled every part of me that was empty from his absence. He smiled before he even ended the kiss. When I looked up into his sparkling hazel eyes, I realised that the first day I'd seen them I'd been a goner. I hadn't even known if he was single then, but somehow I'd been smitten.

"This is our home, Jasmine. I want to live here with you and Bailey and Rose."

"But what about your career? You've worked so hard for it."

His thumbs ran over my cheekbones. "Moving here doesn't mean I have to give it up. It just means it will look different."

"What do you mean?"

He swiped his lips over mine. "I can teach classes online. Two Australian universities have expressed interest. I can work with you as a ranger during tourist season and can conduct research for the National Park Service or the university when I'm free."

"Is that even possible?"

"It is. I've already arranged it. They told me they'd been re-evaluating the resourcing here, and they were going to employ a full-time ranger, so me only working during tourist season suits them."

They hadn't told me that.

"What about your brother and grandparents?"

"They support me. I can still visit. They can visit."

"Will it be enough for you?" I needed to hear the words. I needed to make sure this was what he wanted. I held my breath, waiting for the answer.

"You are enough for me. You are everything." He released me and reached into his pocket. He pulled out a small box and opened it. "Jasmine, will you marry me?"

I stared at the ring. Silver. Swirls like ocean waves encircling a stone the colour of the bay. I pulled the ring out. On the inner surface, the words *love is us* were inscribed. I adored it as much as I adored him.

I handed the ring to Ethan who was studying me. Then I held out my hand. "Absolutely."

He grinned as he slid the ring on my finger. "You had me worried."

"You never need to be worried about my love for you. It's as eternal as the ocean." I flung my arms around his neck and kissed him. Then I took his hand and led him towards home. "We have two hours before the kids come home."

"Good. We have months to make up for."

As soon as we entered the door, Ethan spun me around to face him. He unzipped my jacket and peeled it off my shoulders. His hands following the sleeves left shivers along my skin. He started to undo the buttons of my shirt. This was taking too long. I slapped his hand away, grabbed the hem of my shirt and pulled it over my head. I made similar speed with my bra.

Before I could get any further, Ethan pulled me against him. His strong hands rested on my bare skin as his lips made their way across my collarbone to my neck. Tingles spread through me.

"I missed you so much," he said.

I pulled away and stepped back, undoing my boots. Then I turned and undid my pants while I walked. "Are you coming?"

I glanced over my shoulder. Ethan was following, stripping as he walked. He caught up to me and wrapped his arm around my waist, slowing my pace. When we reached the bed, he stopped. One hand went to my breast, teasing it the way he loved to do. The way I loved him to do. I pushed myself against him. His hard dick pressed into me.

Ethan's other hand made its way between my legs, his fingers rubbing and playing. My breath quickened. He kissed my neck. How was he so coordinated?

"You're so wet."

I moaned, opened my legs, and pushed myself against his hand.

"You want more?" he asked.

What was more? Fingers. Tongue. Dick. I wanted it all. I nodded.

Ethan pushed me onto the bed. "Higher."

I scrambled up the bed. Ethan followed, his fingers inside me instantly. He stuck another one in and pumped. Tightness spread through my body. I raised my hips, increasing the friction. His thumb pressed against my clit, rubbing in time with his fingers. Tightness turned to shaking. Ethan's fingers were relentless. Shaking turned into convulsions. I threw my head back and cried out.

My convulsions subsided. Ethan didn't wait for them to stop. His dick replaced his fingers. He pumped hard and fast. I tried to catch my breath. I couldn't. I cried out again as another orgasm swept through me. Ethan rode me through it. My fingers dug into his back. Unbelievable. How could sex get any better?

Ethan grunted as my hips met his thrust for thrust. His shoulders tensed first. Then his back. His hips lost momentum. I kept mine going. His breath caught and his whole body stiffened. We stopped pumping altogether. Only his dick moved.

I soaked up the sound as a moan mixed with a grunt expanded his chest. Harsh breathing followed. He must have been holding his breath. Ethan kissed me, sloppy and quick, before rolling off me. The winter air was cool against my sweating skin. I never knew a man having an orgasm was so freaking hot.

I reached for his hand. "How could I say no to marrying *Sex on Legs*?"

He chuckled. "OQ would never say no."

CHAPTER SIXTY

Ethan

I stood up as the car made its way toward the house and pulled into the driveway. I walked down the porch stairs, and Rose flung her door open even before Jasmine's car came to a full stop. Seconds later, she was launching herself at me, clinging tight. Her sobs shook her whole body. I held her against me, stroking her hair.

Bailey came next, wrapping his arms around both of us. He was more restrained than his sister, but his arms were no less tight. I kissed the top of his head.

"Are you staying this time?" Bailey asked.

"Your ocean is my ocean."

He squeezed me tighter. Rose squirmed out of our grip. She ran to Jasmine, wrapping her arms around her waist, looking up into Jasmine's face and smiling. "We can be a real family now, together again."

"We sure can," Jasmine said.

Bailey led me inside. "Do you want to see my assignment?"

"I'd love to."

"I'll go get it."

Rose sat at the table. "It's a huge poster. We have to put it in the broom cupboard every night to keep it hidden from Timmy. I think Bailey would lose his shit if it got destroyed."

I raised my eyebrows at her and tried not to laugh at her phrase, even if it was amusing coming from a nine-year-old. I waited for her to reconsider her statement.

Rose pursed her lips and nodded. "Bailey would be distraught if Timmy ruined it."

I smiled. Her word usage was humorous. "That's better. A new favourite word?"

She nodded. "Mummy was upset when you left, but upset is a very boring word. Everyone uses it. So I looked in the thesaurus you gave me for Christmas. Distraught was a much better word."

"I was distraught too, in here." I pointed to my heart.

Bailey appeared with a roll of paper. He rolled it out. It was at least four feet by six feet. He'd drawn a dissection of an ocean scene—the sand stretching out to the ocean, the world below the surface of the water and above it. I studied the drawings. Crabs under the sand through to birds in the sky.

I put my arm around Bailey's shoulders. "This is excellent work."

"Do you think you can help me make sure I got everything?"

"Sure can."

"He also needs to do a report on the ecosystem," Jasmine said.

"You're an expert on reports," Rose said. "You did one to become a doctor, or was it a professor? It doesn't matter.

Mum said your report was hundreds of pages long. And you were busy making it perfect. That's why you couldn't ring."

"Yes, that's right."

Rose wasn't that talkative when we spoke online, but she sure made up for it now.

"Remember the first night you stayed with us? We had my favourite meal then. I think we should have your favourite tonight."

"That's a good idea, Rose," Jasmine said. "Why don't you help me with dinner while Ethan helps Bailey with his assignment?"

Rose left her seat. "We need to do my home reading first."

"We can do it in your room."

Rose giggled as she followed her mum. "Was I giving Ethan an earbashing?"

Jasmine laughed. "You were giving everyone an earbashing."

Bailey and I looked at each other and smiled. As a family, we fit together perfectly.

EPILOGUE

Jasmine

BAILEY, Rose and I sat in the audience with Ethan's family. Rose was sitting between his Gran and Gramps, chatting away. They were nodding and asking her questions.

Bailey sat beside me, studying the auditorium and the audience. "This university is bigger than Somewhere Bay," he said.

Steve laughed. "That's a strange name for a town."

I smiled. "That's Australian sense of humour for you. Where are you? Somewhere. It's a bay. Somewhere Bay."

"That's your closest town, isn't it?" Steve asked.

Bailey nodded. "That's where I go to school. It's forty kilometres from home."

"How far is forty kilometres?" asked Harley.

"Around 25 miles," Steve said.

Harley leant forward with wide eyes to address Bailey. "Your mom has to drive you there every day?"

Bailey shook his head. "Mum drives us to the bus stop. We catch the bus to school."

"Cool. How many kids go there?" Harley asked.

"Around 300."

Harley's eyes nearly popped out of his head. "We have over 2,000 at our school."

Since I'd been here, I understood why Ethan preferred life in Haven Bay for Bailey and Rose. It was hectic here. Traffic was insane. It took us an hour just to travel a short distance. I couldn't imagine doing it every day. And as I looked out the car window I noticed tents in the street, or people lying on the footpaths. Their eyes were empty, staring into nothingness. Everything was expensive. No wonder there were so many homeless.

The auditorium quieted down as a school official came to the microphone. Rose stared raptly at the stage. Bailey sat taller.

We watched as Ethan's row of students stood and walked to the back of the hall to the opposite side, dressed in black robes. What they wore on their feet told their story. Some were in dress shoes like Ethan, others were in work boots and others in sneakers.

Ethan gave Bailey a wink as he walked past. I don't know how he was so calm. Butterflies were beating their wings in my stomach. I watched him all the way to the opposite side where he met his mentor, Lloyd.

One by one, the candidates went up on stage. By the time Ethan's turn came, my hands were sweating. Ethan and Lloyd walked on stage together. My throat tightened as I tried to hold my tears in. Ethan's name was announced. He turned away from Lloyd, who placed the royal blue hood over his head. He faced Lloyd who pulled Ethan in for a hug. They separated, both smiling at each other.

He'd done it. Everything he'd worked so hard for was finally accomplished. We all clapped, Bailey the loudest in our group. I wiped at my tears. I hoped the waterproof mascara lived up to its promise.

When the ceremony was over, we went into the reception hall. Ethan was chatting to Lloyd and glancing at the door, waiting for us. He smiled broadly when he spotted us. Rose ran ahead and embraced him. Bailey was next.

"Are these your biggest fans?" Lloyd asked.

Ethan chuckled. "They're my biggest everything."

Lloyd addressed Bailey and Rose. "You must be very proud of Ethan."

Rose nodded as she gazed up into Ethan's face. "One day Bailey is going to be just like him."

"Not you?"

"No. I don't like writing long, boring reports."

Lloyd laughed. "It's not for all of us." He considered Bailey. "A future doctor, are you?"

Bailey nodded. "Dad will be my mentor."

Ethan's eyes widened ever so slightly. He pulled Bailey into a side hug. Fresh tears sprang into my eyes.

I approached Ethan and gave him a peck. "Congratulations."

"This must be the woman who stole you away from me," Lloyd said.

I shook his hand. "I don't know if it was me, the children or the sea lions."

Ethan grinned. "You were first."

"Good answer," Lloyd said before excusing himself.

I sidled up to Ethan. "When exactly did you lose the battle?"

"When I saw you on your front porch and you reminded me of the ocean."

"The ocean?"

"Wildly beautiful."

THANK you for reading Seal of Approval. If you would like to join Jasmine and Ethan on their wedding day please click here for the bonus epilogue or alternatively type in https://dl.bookfunnel.com/n6g2z7wcef.

KEEP IN TOUCH

To be notified of future releases, and to keep up to date with other news, please join my newsletter.

https://www.subscribepage.com/p9p9y0

OTHER books available in the Love Down Under Series are:

<u>The Cat's Out of the Bag</u>

She's started a new life. He's escaping his. Can two tortured souls find a future together?

Evie's a survivor. After rebuilding herself and her life, she's feeling the one thing she never thought she would – happy.

Until Jesse...

When she meets Jesse while volunteering at a cat shelter, dark memories of her past return. She is stronger now and wants to trust him, but after all she's been through, is trust even possible?

Jesse's a self-made billionaire yearning to get away from his empty life and the money-hungry parasites who inhabit it.

The plan?

Go to sunny Australia, leaving his old life behind, to find himself. But instead of finding just himself, he finds Evie, who is everything anyone should aspire to be. Now, what he aspires to be, is hers.

But to be hers, he needs to tell her everything and putting his heart on the line is hard.

The quest to find a cat a forever home leads them to travel across the country together. Will they find the strength to confide in each other? Or will the close quarters drive them apart?

When she left him…

…Tara couldn't explain why.

After five years, did she still have feelings for Shepherd?

Her brother's passing hit Tara hard and it left a scar. That night, at the party, when she saw Shepherd high, Tara had no choice, it was over. It brought up too many painful memories and she wouldn't go through it again. The decision was simple.

She had to leave.

No goodbye.

For Shepherd, losing Tara broke his heart. Not knowing why she left, well that pain he addressed with drugs, alcohol, and meaningless relationships. After he hit rock bottom, he cleaned up and came up with a plan to get her back. Could it work?

It was his only shot.

Would a desperate ruse, with the best intentions, but costing a fortune, give him the chance to win her heart for good? Or would it ruin him?

Will she be brave enough to be loved?

<u>Get Off Your High Horse</u>

When two opposites collide will their differences ignite a spark?

Frankie and Sebastian live totally different lives. Lives that are entwined through polo, the sport of kings. How entangled will they become?

Australian farmgirl, Frankie, has no interest in high society or the rich, arrogant riders she has to deal with, especially Sebastian. Her heart may be softening to his kindness and love of horses, but her brain won't be convinced. She's looking forward to her summer break on the farm, away from him...

...until her parents invite Sebastian to stay.

Sebastian never felt comfortable in his role as the Crown Prince of Oleander. He'd rather spend his days working with horses, playing polo and being with Frankie, whose fiery spirit has set his heart aflame.

But pressure from his mother, the Queen, to return to his royal duties is mounting. Everything he desires is in danger of being ripped away.

Can Sebastian convince Frankie that his hopes and dreams aren't so different from hers, or is he destined to return to a life he doesn't want, alone?

Love and secrets are a tricky combination

For Emily, going home isn't easy, especially when her small town never felt like home in the first place. She escaped Alma seven years ago when she went to university, but now her estranged father needs her help. At least returning means spending time with the only good thing in town—her best friend, Luke.

Luke always knew Emily needed to be free of their hometown, so he withheld his true feelings. Even though she has returned, he knows she will never stay. He tries hard to respect the boundaries of their friendship but every moment they spend together makes it harder to deny their connection. Self-control dissipates. One kiss turns into two...

But is Luke really the man Emily remembers? When Emily discovers Luke has betrayed her trust, they could lose the most precious thing of all—each other.

<u>A Bird in the Hand</u>

**She yearns for the past. He wants a better future.
Can they learn to love the present together?**

When thirty-something Makayla's long-term boyfriend breaks it off, she is left broken hearted. Her best friends seize the opportunity and book a bus tour up the west coast of Australia. They hope distance will give her perspective, but she can't see past what she's lost.

Tyler needs a break from work and seeks something more fulfilling, even if he has no idea what that is. When his mates plan the trip of a lifetime he decides to tag along. He's sure it will get him out of his rut, and in turn, help him set a course for his future.

No one is prepared for the planning mishap that finds Makayla and Tyler sharing a room. They are opposites in just about every way and are definitely not interested in each other. Add a fouled mouthed cockatoo to the equation and the perfect trip is not so perfect. Or is it?

Eight years apart hasn't made her heart grow fonder…

Clare Walker is a third-generation company woman. *Hart Apples* saved her family from destitution and now it's her turn to return the favour. Work is her one true love, leaving no room for anything – or anyone – else. She knows what the company needs to survive another generation, and it's not the owner's son—her ex-best friend, the annoying and attractive, Beau Hart.

Beau returns to his family orchard after eight years away. He's stronger now and has his mental illness under control. He wants to prove his worth to his family. Most of all, though, he wants to reunite with the only woman he has ever loved, Clare Walker. The first task is difficult, but the second is near impossible, especially as Clare's attitude toward him goes beyond the cold shoulder.

When Beau's father elects them as the company's saviours, Clare's plans of keeping Beau at a distance are thwarted. Now she just needs to keep it all about business…if only those pesky feelings would stay away.

Love can heal the scars on your heart

Lachlan

So what if I've gone through four nannies in three short years? I know what's best for my children and it's not the nanny my mother and ex-wife have hired.

Peyton may be all kinds of beautiful but she is totally unsuitable—city girl, former doctor and no experience.

Problem is, everybody loves her. I don't want to feel the same; one failure at love is enough. Besides, I have a duty to my family and the farm.

Except the more I spend time with her, the more I'm drawn to her honesty and bravery. I need to remember, a farm is no place for a woman like Peyton; she will not stay.

Peyton

After an accident put an end to my surgical career, I jumped at the opportunity to be a nanny. Moving to Australia will get me away from my controlling family. It's time I start making my own decisions.

But falling for my boss is not the wisest one I could make, even if it feels right. It doesn't hurt that his singing makes my panties melt.

Everything is perfect—I feel heard and seen for the first time (and I don't just mean my scars).

I'm where I belong...until my family get involved. Then I'm left with no job and no home.

Now I need to make the biggest decision of all—stand up to my family, choose my happy and fight for love.

ACKNOWLEDGMENTS

Cover by Amanda Walker PA & Design Services
Edited by Empowered Writing
Proofread by Half Caff Press
And thanks to my amazing beta readers

ABOUT THE AUTHOR

Cynthia is a Document Controls Manager by day and an author by night. She believes in happily ever afters and positive relationships. She enjoys writing about places she visited with her daughter while they travelled around Australia. She says that travel and reading are the best educators. A love of animals sees them feature in her books, some have small parts, others larger.

Find her online: http://cynthiaterelst.com/

All of her social links can be found here, Linktree: https://linktr.ee/cynthiaterelst

www.ingramcontent.com/pod-product-compliance
Lightning Source LLC
Chambersburg PA
CBHW030603120726
47904CB00006B/1752